VOLITION

A GOTHIC TALE

JOHN H. HILTON

Jan-Carol
Publishing, Inc

"every story needs a book"

Volition: A Gothic Tale
John H. Hilton
Published October 2025
Little Creek Books
Imprint of Jan-Carol Publishing, Inc.
All rights reserved
Copyright © 2025 John H. Hilton
Title page image: © Fantasy Maps/Adobe Stock
Cover design: Tara Sizemore

ISBN: 978-1-962561-98-3
Library of Congress Control Number: On file

You may contact the publisher:
Jan-Carol Publishing, Inc.
PO Box 701
Johnson City, TN 37605
publisher@jancarolpublishing.com
www.jancarolpublishing.com

To Claudia,
I am proud to be your sidekick!

Also by John H. Hilton

Cloth and Dagger

PREFACE

In our day, the best of literature makes a suggestion to the author—that his or her characters be a mixed bag of virtue and vice, of elevated principles and flexible operational mores—for the insightful reader craves a degree of psychological complexity in a story and its persons. Without such, the whole enterprise is flat and might not be worth the read. Thus, the complete story should elucidate the frightening range of passions that motivate strong-willed individuals and the distance they are prepared to go in their pursuit. Weak-willed individuals and those who have no idea what they want (much less how to get it) should receive some treatment as well, since these folks tend to comprise the majority of the population.

When a young man and his cohorts achieve unusual prowess in their dealings, they begin to view themselves as superior to other men, superior to the world around them. These men, particularly their leader, are on the cusp of achieving something quite large and dark. A young judge, with a handful of dutiful subordinates, is directing events to suit his own ends, bending reality to his will. As he seems to win at every turn, gaining everything he desires, the game takes on heightened significance. Power and will attempt to exact a price from our young judge. Will he be done in by his Nietzschean Superman? Will he morph into moral submission, seeking redemption? Or will he up the ante on everyone and everything around him, continuing to give the world a swift and well-deserved kick in the ass?

We know what Lord Acton said about power corrupting men. But what if, in the judge's case, wealth, prestige, and power—as we in the present day have come to understand it—is not his ultimate goal? Modern psychology studies people and attempts to classify their behavior and motivations. But there are some few individuals who are never easily classified, let alone understood. And since we never see them coming until it is too late, they occupy space in a small and elite group of human beings; the dangerous and seemingly indestructible.

It is no accident that our story takes place in the hill country in Virginia, the oldest and most historic state in America. Someone once said that the "hills have eyes." The hills also produce men of uncommon strength, savvy, and willpower. Unlike people in the cities, mountain folks are shrouded in perpetual mystery. They are consequential and they endure, like the land and the fearsome predatory mammals that roam these Virginia hills. Yes, the hills have a spirit all their own and continually produce the most valiant and durable men. Allow me to take you on a journey featuring a few of them. It may be an illuminating experience, or perhaps, something entirely different.

A short time ago, a vocationally undistinguished and morally ambiguous attorney became a judge in a Virginia High Court. Judge John P. Devereaux (Jack) was only 35 years old when he took his seat as the newest and youngest member of the Fauquier County Circuit Court. The appointment came none too soon. His father had begun the process of changing his will, disinheriting his son who had offended him one too many times. Over the objections of Jack's doting mother, the young man would be rendered penniless. The only son of

Thomas and Corrine Devereaux would be cut out of a vast family fortune which spanned four generations.

Heated arguments between the parents extended well into the night, with Mrs. Devereaux pleading a hopeless case for her son. The parents had given their boy everything. Jack grew up on a spectacular estate, frolicking on the farm and in the wilderness and attending the best schools. His wits and charm got him through college and law school, but his work ethic was lax. Like so many aristocratic families in Virginia, he was pressured to marry a young lady whom his parents and their society approved. His father staked him in his own local law practice, with the expectation that he would labor for more hours than there are in a day and focus on corporate and commercial cases, thereby making for himself the reputation that his father enjoyed as a premier corporate lawyer.

All this did Jack Devereaux have at the tender age of 25. But 10 years passing saw all the expectations of a prideful and imperious father shattered. Instead of using his considerable privilege and good fortune to make his family proud, he squandered his time and legal talents working at his own leisure, taking cases representing friends and girl-friends who got into trouble. And the wife who had so elevated Jack's reputation filed for divorce and took an undisclosed settlement from Mr. Devereaux.

Jack continued, however, to use his legal practice to court favor from wealthy socialites in the Piedmont region and enjoyed unsurpassed popularity. Invited to no less than six social gatherings a week, he always arrived with a different lady on his arm. It was not long before most of the county discovered what Jack's father had already known—that his divorce had little to do with anything other than his serial adultery. But his extensive socializing and doing favors for prominent people paid off at the most critical juncture. One day, a brilliant courtroom success led to the gratitude of a certain state senator, who in turn recommended Jack Devereaux for a judgeship on the Circuit Court, despite his reputation as a playboy and questionable professional. His troubles abruptly reversed; his mother would now have more ammunition to fire at her husband. What legal family wouldn't take pride in having their young son sitting on a high court?

Jack speculated that his father would have to stand down on his threat to change his will. In this case, that speculation paid off. Thomas Devereaux backed away from the disinheritance, but for one stipulation. The appointed court term lasted nine years, being subject to reappointment by the General Assembly of Virginia. Devereaux' s professional and personal conduct would be under the scrutiny of the State Bar Association, and the state police and local authorities. If his son could display exemplary behavior and be reappointed to the Court nine years hence, then he would remain one of three heirs of the Devereaux fortune, estimated at some $3.5 billion. His two sisters, the younger one married, the older one single, would receive the other two-thirds of the estate. So, it appears that cleverness and good fortune supplanted duty and diligence, and Jack Devereaux would have it all very shortly. And shortly thereafter, tragedy would strike.

Set in the mystical and magical world of Virginia's Piedmont region at the foothills of the Blue Ridge Mountains, our story unfolds within a community of unimaginable beauty, wealth, and southern eccentricity. A pastoral paradise where the well-to-do do as they please, and in an air of exquisite privacy. A place with very little crime as compared with the urban areas, yet one needn't look too far to find evil lurking about, seeking to devour oblivious prey. Not the evil of fairy tales or that deplored in religious texts. But rather the evil that manifests itself in the wretchedness of the human condition. For in the end, that is where the battle between the light and darkness plays out; and there are few guarantees. Those readers who are perpetually optimistic about human nature are advised to abandon some hope as they navigate through this labyrinthine tale.

VOLUME ONE

"I am an aristocrat. I love liberty; I hate equality."

— Senator John Randolph, Virginia

CHAPTER I

Thomas Devereaux, I will not let you ruin our son. You will cease this will changing at once," scolded the protective mother.

"He has ruined himself, and nearly all of us in the process, Corrine," Thomas said. "There is something dark in his character! He cares nothing for what is important in life."

"He got a good education, he went to law school as you directed, and he is a practicing attorney, just as you told him to be," Mrs. Devereaux insisted.

"Corrine! I will have no more of this. His conduct has been nothing short of disgraceful. Honor demands a separation."

"You will leave him with nothing, Thomas?" exploded an angry Mrs. Devereaux.

"With his moral fiber, or more accurately the lack thereof, he would whittle away any fortune we bequeathed him anyway. It's time to take the bull by the balls. As of next week, our son is on his own."

Corrine threw her scotch glass at the fireplace mantle and stormed upstairs to the bedroom. Mr. Devereaux noticed the glass did not break. He picked it up and poured himself a drink and retired to the guest bedroom.

The next morning, the Devereauxs were paid a visit by their son. "Jack, do sit down and eat something. Coffee?" asked Mrs. Devereaux.

"Sure, Mom, thanks."

Corrine went for the coffee and food, leaving Jack's scowling father to hopefully engage in civil conversation. It was not to be had. As Thomas started in on Jack, the son presented a formal letter from the Senator—and Virginia House Speaker—informing him that a vote on his appointment to the Virginia Circuit Court Fauquier, Rappahannock, and Culpeper Counties would be held that Friday morning. No objections having been filed or voiced, his ascension to the highest municipal court would be a *fait accompli.*

"Surely, Pop, you would not embarrass the only judge in our family with a messy little thing like inheritance," chimed in a confident and smug Jack.

Corrine offered affectionate congratulations, while Thomas sat at the table in disbelief that any state official would entrust his son to a judgeship. "You and your father need to bury the hatchet this minute. I am sick to death of the bad blood in this family," Corrine said. Both men in the room began to talk above the other, and Corrine shut them up with, "I don't care who started what, this ends today!"

As Thomas Devereaux continued to scowl, Jack seemed more receptive to his mother's pleas. "Today is Tuesday, three days from your confirmation vote according to your letter. I see no reason not to celebrate in advance. Come to dinner tonight, and your father and I will announce some adjustments concerning your future," Corrine winked at Jack as she spooned a serving of cold eggs onto her husband's plate. "And bring whatever young lady you happen to be spending time with. I do so like that secretary of yours. Yes, bring her, Jack! We will have gobs of claret with the meal, and of course, champagne afterwards."

The young man stood up and thanked his mom with a kiss. He and his father grudgingly shook hands. As he drove away, Jack Devereaux looked in his rear-view mirror and gave himself a wink. "Nice work," he said to himself.

And what a stroke of luck. As a young lawyer who often appeared in court, Jack had fantasized of being a judge, as do most lawyers. But he never took any steps to place himself in the "bull-pin," as they say. When his client, the Senator, mentioned it, he was taken entirely by surprise. But my, how fortunes change! Not only was this playboy attorney about to take his seat at the top of his profession, but he knew beyond any doubt that he would remain his parents' heir, provided he could keep his mouth shut at dinner that evening.

As Jack drove south on State Route 17, he glanced in both directions to view the horse farms. The cool spring morning was overcast with a light mist slowly rising from the ground, accentuating the green grass everywhere. It was reminiscent of the patchwork of meadows and moors in rural England. Devereaux was born and raised in this sublime landscape, his aesthetic sensibilities always heightened like that of people who had lived all of their lives in cities and recently moved to the Virginia Piedmont to be country ladies and gentlemen. Born a country gentleman, not a day went by where Jack did not ingest this treasure of the rural south, nor fail to appreciate its distinguishing characteristics.

As he entered the town of Warrenton, the county seat of Fauquier, he pulled up to his office near the Old Town Historic District, walked in with his usual strut, and greeted his legal secretary. "I brought you coffee and breakfast, courtesy of my mother," he said to a smiling and sharply attractive young woman named Geraldine Pike.

"Why, thank you, Mr. Devereaux. It's nice being your only employee," she said.

"I can barely afford you, Jeri."

The two laughed almost uncontrollably, for she knew nothing of his travails with his father and had always assumed she was working for a trust fund baby. "Close the office tomorrow and for the rest of the week, Jeri. I will pay you for the next three days anyway," Jack said as he handed her the letter from the legislature.

"Oh my, is this for real? A Circuit Court Judge!" The two hugged and kissed each other.

"I don't want any of my weird clients walking in here and fucking up my appointment," Jack said. Then, Jeri grabbed Devereaux by his jacket lapels and planted a deep kiss on him. "I think we will shut down the office early today as well," said Jack as he turned down the blinds on the windows. "Oh, and cancel any plans you might have made for tonight. You're coming home with me for dinner."

CHAPTER 2

The late morning's activities had been delightful but tiring. Devereaux and his assistant had retired to their respective residences to rest up for the late evening that was upon them. If true to form, the drinking would last well into the night and both he and Jeri would pack a bag being ready to stay over at the Devereaux Mansion back up the state road in Markham. It had happened before. Jeri had been Jack's secretary for just under two years, and this impossibly gorgeous and witty young lady had charmed the paint right off the walls of the manor house on her last visit, endearing herself to Corrine Devereaux. Thomas, who didn't approve of anything his son did, was grudgingly stupefied with Jack's choice of legal secretary. Her presence in his house was the only time anyone got to see a little life and giddiness express itself in the old man.

As the pretty pair turned into the long and winding driveway, Jack pressed a button, and a most imposing black iron gate opened. They passed through this not terribly subtle security apparatus and up a slight incline toward the mansion, which Thomas Devereaux had named Bourbon Hill— less of a reference to the whiskey than to his supposed loose ancestry to the Bourbon Royal Dynasty of France. A history major in college, Jack delighted in tormenting his father with the fact that the Devereaux clan originated from Normandy and some of them most likely followed King William in the 1066 A.D. invasion of England. Many Normans were direct descendants of Danish Vikings who had invaded the area a century or two before. Jack missed few opportunities to remind his father that he had a better claim to English or Scandinavian royalty than French. And those claims were somewhat lame as well.

"Should I lead off with the delusions of grandeur my dad still harbors as a French Aristocrat?"

Jeri giggled as she squeezed Jack's muscular right arm. "Why don't you wait until you have everything you want before taunting your poor father. Really, Jack. Everyone but you considers him to be a very fine and gracious gentleman."

"That's the problem, my dear. Pop has a special unpleasant side that is reserved entirely for me."

The Devereaux Estate was spectacular by any standards, and at twilight it was otherworldly. Most of the acreage was wooded and uncultivated, except for the massive front lawn. It being April, every possible color of azalea lined the front and left side of the house. Tulips, lilies, star magnolias, and dogwoods engulfed in a sea of the greenest grass gorgeously highlighted the boxwood outline of the property's frontal boundaries. Of course, the house was French Provincial and seemed to enlarge itself every time Jack paid his folks a visit. Jeri just sat in the car as they parked, staring with her mouth agape at the luxurious display.

Jack whisked his paramour over to a leafed-out maple tree and spent a few minutes reminding her of why she was crazy about him. It had nothing at all to do with the big house. Well...maybe a little. "I think I love you, Jack Devereaux! Please be gentle and kind," whispered Jeri.

Jack picked her up, swung her around and around, observing nothing else than her joyful and wonderfully dimpled expressions. "I can't do without you either. Let's see, by nightfall I predict you will repeat yourself, but without the word 'think.' Now, let's go inside and get drunk."

"Okay, you naughty boy," Jeri proclaimed.

"As I told you the last time we were here, drunk is not just the best way to spend time with my dad—it's the *only* way," Jack replied.

"Welcome, Miss Geraldine, you beautiful young thing," a gracious Mrs. Devereaux said as she grabbed Jeri's hands and kissed her on both cheeks. All smiles, Jeri urged Corrine to call her by her nickname. But Corrine reminded Jeri that her favorite aunt was named Geraldine. "Okay, then. Geraldine it is."

* * *

As the Devereauxs and their distinguished guest wined and dined themselves into a mild stupor, some clandestinely sketchy things were happening less than 20 miles away in the charming and historical hamlet of Upperville. Luxury cars and SUVs were turning off State Highway 50 (which serves as Main Street in Upperville) and slowly and carefully parking under tree cover on the massive lot of the Fauquier County Horse Show grounds. This abundance of acreage would be teeming with activity in the subsequent months of June and July, but for now they were closed. It was the perfect place to park undiscovered and undisturbed for the men who exited their vehicles and quickly walked across Main Street into a section of woods where they disappeared from all notice. Some moments later, a small clearing in the woods produced an old Victorian House with yellow Stucco walls. Unlit from outside, dim lights were noticeable on the first floor and in what had to be bedrooms on the second.

Two gentlemen were making their way to the front porch as another gentleman on his way out hugged and pawed at the statuesque and magnificent female figure at the door. The woman laughed and gave the drunken man a gentle shove, and he left. As the two visitors hit the porch, the gorgeous woman, not recognizing one of them, asked for the password.

"Password," cried the man. "I plum forgot it."

The woman hiked up her leather skirt even higher than it was and gave the man a wicked laugh. "No password, no dessert, sweet thing," she said.

"Damn, damn! I've got to get in that house and have a drink and a poke," he said as he looked at the other man. "I can't leave, I just can't. I can't go home to my wife and kids unless I get some ass right the fuck now."

The other man chuckled, as he understood precisely how the tipsy fellow felt and tried to help him. "Now, just think for a minute. The password is two words. In fact, it is the name of a place."

The drunk man scratched his head. "It's on the tip of my tongue, but I can't..."

"One more hint is all she is going to let me give you, my friend. It comes straight out of a Faulkner novel. Think."

The poor inebriated soul sat on the porch and feverishly began to rattle off names in his head. Just as he started to cry in abject frustration, he turned to the woman and said, "Frenchmen's Bend."

"Welcome to The Lounge for the well-to-do," said Miss Mimi. "You are well-to-do, I hope?"

"Oh yes, ma'am. I'm a banker out of Winchester and I'm a gentleman. My apologies for my coarse and vulgar language, but I get that way when I've had a little to drink and when I'm climbing the walls for some first class—"

"I think we get the picture, my friend," the other man said. "You go inside while I speak with the lady of the house."

No banker from Winchester was ever so happy to be entering a house of ill repute as our weepy friend! The second man walked up to Miss Mimi and whispered Frenchman's Bend in her ear as he gently squeezed her butt cheek. "Where's Kelly Ann?" inquired the man.

"She's in the back bar," exclaimed Mimi. "By the way, Mr. Devereaux called earlier. He said it's time to change the password."

* * *

Back in Markham, the party at Bourbon Hill were enjoying the cool evening on the veranda drinking Tawny Port. Thomas Devereaux had predictably succumbed to the machinations of his wife and son—to distinguish himself on the bench and be reappointed in nine years to a second term as a judge. Then, young Jack would remain in the will unmodified. Thomas had struggled with irritating thoughts all evening; those of his son and the idea that his wife would bring up family business in front of a near stranger. But Jeri's charms and an absurd number of libations softened him up, and Jack and his mother achieved every goal.

Pleased with himself and holding Jeri's hand while telling off-color jokes to his three dining mates, Jack felt his phone vibrate in his coat pocket. "Excuse me, everyone, just a little client business. I'll be right back."

Jack dialed the number as he went inside the house. "Mimi."

"Well, hey there, Mr. Devereaux, what a fine evening it is. And even finer to hear your voice. Business is so good today, except everyone seems to be getting some but me. Come down here later and I..."

"I'm tied up with family tonight, honey, but I'll come and see you tomorrow afternoon before you open," said a pleasantly distracted Jack. "The new password is *Bench Warrant*. Got it, Madame?"

"Got it, stud muffin."

"You know, Mimi, I get such a kick out of calling you Madame, having it apply personally and professionally."

"You bad boy! I'm going to powder my bottom special, the way you like."

"Seriously, I have something to tell you tomorrow. It requires absolute secrecy. And wear the aqua-colored mini dress. I'm sweating cold right now just imagining," he exclaimed.

"Anything for you, beautiful man. Come by at 3 p.m."

"Will do. Nighty night," Jack said. "Well, don't those clients just come in all interesting shapes and sizes," he exclaimed as he reclaimed his seat on the porch.

Jack drank and smiled the smile of victory, scoring a double whammy at both Bourbon Hill and in that other place. He knew that nothing in the short term could clip his rising stock.

* * *

The next morning, Devereaux was admiring himself in the mirror behind the door to his office. The blinds were all pulled, as he did not want anyone coming inside until the following week, after his confirmation vote. As he had entered his 30s, Jack had expected with a sense of dread that his good looks would slowly begin to decline. At age 35, he was pleasantly surprised to be even more handsome than ever. The lines on his face combined with his hair turning slightly gray gave him the distinguished look of a vintage movie actor, a professor, or the gentleman professional he already was. He was, in reality, a practiced gentleman rake, a lifestyle he picked up in his last year of high school and developed so superbly that he easily fit right into the English society novel, or the modern soap opera. Still in excellent physical shape, Jack kept his six-foot-three, 220-pound frame buffed, sculpted, and eminently proportional.

In college and the years following, he religiously practiced two sports: weightlifting and fencing. The combination of the two gave him maximum strength and coordination skill, not to mention elevating his already pronounced swashbuckling quality. In high school, he had been an accomplished tight end on the football team and one of the finest baseball players in the northern part of the state.

However, any hopes of an athletic career were dashed by his college athletic director, who told him he wasn't big enough to play football as an end or linebacker. When baseball season hit, he was insulted to be placed as a second string first baseman in favor of a senior. This, even though Jack could field as well and at bat could hit better. Had he stayed with baseball two years he might have amounted to something. But that was not his style. Deferred gratification was difficult for Jack. He resigned himself to the gym and activities that he could do himself as opposed to team sports.

Jack Devereaux was not a man who indulged in recriminations or regrets. He was a man of the moment. Stewing over his past, engaging in journeys of self-discovery, and torturous character building were silly and useless to him. Rather, how to enjoy himself in the extreme and use his talents to get what he wanted had seized his psyche long ago. As he contemplated the flash-backs from days gone by, Jack went to the bathroom sink, splashed water on his hair, and combed it back. He wanted to see if the hair appeared any less gray when wet.

"You log more mirror time than I do, or any of my girlfriends, for that matter," said Jeri as she surprised a tediously distracted Devereaux.

"What are you doing here? I closed up shop, remember?"

"I know. I had lunch with my friend Emily Tarkington and saw your car," said a playful Geraldine.

"I can't decide whether to admire or mourn these gray hairs," he said.

"Didn't you once tell me that you made a deal with God that if you didn't lose your hair, you would never complain about the color?"

"Yes, I did, and I intend to keep my part, but this all your fault, Jeri," Jack said teasingly.

"My fault?"

"Indeed! Now that I'm in love with you, I can't have you admiring another man's looks more than mine."

"Jack Devereaux, you are both wonderful and stupid."

"Stupid?"

"You finally tell me you love me in this backhanded way, and then you make it all about your male ego...You're insufferable," Jeri said as she moved seductively into Jack's space. Putting her arms around his neck, she told him that he was the most dashing and sexy man she'd ever met. Jack just stood there mollified and slightly embarrassed as Jeri sat down at her desk to make a phone call.

He had just told Jeri that he loved her. Something they both had known for some time and something that she had told him first. Jeri looked over at him with tears of joy welling up in her big gorgeous brown eyes. As she put down the phone, she told Jack that her high opinion of him would be up for regular reevaluation depending on his treatment of her. It was an amazing moment for them both. Jack gave Jeri and easy smile, but he knew she meant business. He would endeavor to engulf her with his affections and appreciation and never take her for granted. This would be relatively easy, but of course there was that other thing that might not be.

Geraldine was 31 years old and a local girl. She had been a legal secretary since graduating high school in Warrenton. Her father was a retired Master Sergeant in the Army, a white southerner from the mountains near Asheville, North Carolina. Her mother was a stunning beauty from Savannah, Georgia, who met her husband when he was stationed nearby. She was ethnically mixed, African American, and white. They had divorced some years back and made feeble attempts to get along for their daughter's sake. Now, imagine: Jeri was five-foot-nine and did some plus-size modeling in her 20s. Her curly dark brown hair unfolded down to her waist and her ultra smooth, cream-colored skin combined with the most voluptuous and curvaceous figure carrying such a potently accentuated bosom that upon sight, a man froze into a gravitational pull of desire. One's eyes could only be distracted away by her equally fabulous thick legs and derrière. Jack, being a tall and fairly large man, was quite compatible with the luscious Geraldine. And besides, skinny girls never turned him on anyway. When Jeri popped by the office nearly two years prior for an informal job interview, it was *lust at first sight* for our soon-to-be judge.

He would never forget the first time they were intimidate. She completely owned him for those few hours that steamy afternoon. The experience was so intensely hot that he was knocked off his game for perhaps the first time in his life. She eventually came to work for him, and Devereaux grew to be smitten with her charm, wit, and what he came to appreciate the most—her oversupply of affection and loyalty towards him.

Jeri, of course, knew nothing about Jack's extra-curricular activities in Upperville; and thus, it would have to remain for now. He trusted her implicitly but would not bear any loss of love or respect from her. Yet, he had unfinished business to wrap up. And not just with Miss Mimi.

CHAPTER 3

Devereaux was often late for appointments, for he could afford his nonchalant ways. But he met Mimi promptly at 3 p.m. at their place of business. "*Bonjour, Jack, tu es un bel homme.*"

Mimi Charleville was French on her mother's side. She had met Jack when she was a real estate agent in her mother's brokerage, and he was the lawyer for most of their closings. Mimi's mother, Isabel, took a liking to the handsome young attorney but endeavored to keep Mimi at a safe distance from him. Her plan was less than successful.

"Come upstairs, *amour*. It's been a while since you paid proper attention to me," said the seductress.

"All powdered up, my dear?" Jack inquired as he followed her up the stairs, licking his lips.

Almost two hours later, Jack woke up from a power nap. He looked over at Mimi, who was in and out of sleep. Then he looked at his watch. The girls, the piano player, and the bartender were due to arrive any moment and begin the evening's festivities. "Mimi, wake up," he said.

"Ummm, Jack! That was well worth the wait," she said.

"You need to get downstairs, and I need to leave," Jack exclaimed.

Mimi followed instructions, and as Devereaux got dressed he smacked himself upside the head, for in all that heat and subsequent slumber he had forgotten to talk with Mimi about his judicial appointment. Jack chased Mimi down the stairs, poured them both a scotch, and led her outside.

"A judge. Here in Fauquier! Why, Mr. Devereaux, you never cease to amaze."

"It all goes down on Friday. We need to meet Sunday night to discuss some particulars. Close the house at 8 p.m."

"Yes, sir," said Mimi as she jokingly saluted Jack. "But my little old feelings will be mighty hurt if I'm the last one to know this thrilling news."

"No, darling, you're the first. Except for McSherry. I told him right away. Now, not a word of this to anyone. Not staff, not clients, nobody."

"Got it. Thank you for a...most titillating afternoon." Jack kissed Mimi on the lips and left in a hurry.

* * *

Devereaux zipped back to his office to grab his briefcase and some computer discs, and then it would be home to read a while and get some more sleep. Friday afternoon would be upon him, and he didn't want any boats rocked. He noticed Jeri's car outside, and when he walked into the office, he saw her working diligently at her computer.

"You and I are not even supposed to be here, sweetheart," Jack said.

"Oh, I need the big computer to do what I'm doing now," said Jeri.

"And what might that be?" Jack put his hands on Jeri's shoulders and kissed the top of her head.

"Doing the graphics for your invitations."

"What invitations?"

"For the party that I'm going to throw you. I've enlisted your mother's help, too." Jack hugged Jeri from behind, holding onto her a little too long. Perhaps a combination of love and guilt in the works. Miss Pike stood virtually alone in her capacity to produce any remorseful feelings in Devereaux.

He was not naturally prone to the "useless emotion," as he called it. He was overwhelmed by her gesture which was not at all out of character for the very thoughtful secretary.

Now, for a brief pause, dear reader. This author believes that there are men out there who do not deserve the love of such a woman as Geraldine Pike. And he is beginning to wonder if Mr. Devereaux is one of those men. Alas, Devereaux is a step or two ahead of us. For he knows beyond a shadow of a doubt that he does not deserve such a lady as she. Be he will strive to keep her anyway. We are dealing with a man who is not altogether devoid of morals and benevolent emotions. But he seldom, if ever, allowed them to get in his way.

Friday came, and Jack went to Jeri's place to drink and watch the General Assembly session on TV. Jeri cradled her lover in her arms, who was now beginning to sweat nervously as the votes were taken in the State Senate. His nomination had been confirmed by a voice vote in the House of Delegates earlier that morning. Jack could not bring himself to admit to Jeri that he was anxious. He wanted to appear self-assured as usual. Jeri knew better. As the proceedings continued, she held him all the tighter. All of a sudden, UNANIMOUS! Devereaux confirmed by the upper house, and Jack would become Judge Devereaux in just a few weeks after his swearing-in ceremony. It was done. A clever but devious and injudicious young lawyer would be a Circuit Judge. He would now wear an imposing black robe and send people to jail. Oh, joy!

"I can hardly believe it, baby, you did it. I'm so proud of you," Jeri exclaimed.

Jack and Geraldine celebrated for the rest of the day and evening at her place. He fielded congratulatory calls from his mother and sister, as well as some fellow attorneys and society friends.

The next day, Saturday, Jeri would be at his place. That particular weekend demanded more sexual stamina from the young judge-to-be than he thought any man could possess. But he pleased himself and his mate quite well, not to mention the positive byproduct of being so physically spent that he would be incapable of giving into the usual urges toward Mimi on Sunday.

Making love to Geraldine was beautiful, loving, red hot, and sizzling. But sex with Mimi had a dirty, nasty quality that Jack found hard to resist, the aforementioned other thing!

Devereaux was all business, however, at The Lounge on Sunday evening at 8 p.m. Before Mimi was ready for the meeting, the man who helped the banker with the password walked in. Frank McSherry was a Detective Sergeant with the Virginia State Police and a most imposing individual. About the same height as Jack, he was broad shouldered, barrel chested, and quicker with his hands than most fighting men around. He could draw and shoot a gun before any poor and unfortunate soul knew what was happening, having learned how to fight growing up in the hills of Eastern Kentucky and serving in the Army before joining the police. Unfortunately for McSherry, the State Police paid little. Fortunately for McSherry, Jack Devereaux paid well. Yes, these three made quite the criminal enterprise. Mimi as the Madame, running a dozen girls; Jack Devereaux as the businessman and lawyer; and McSherry as the muscle and police protection. Devereaux owned the operation outright and took very good care of his people. And they took care of him.

As Mimi came down, the three drank scotch and Jack began to talk. "I've set up a dummy corporation. The girls will continue to be paid in cash, but they will get their health insurance from the new company. Frank is all cash. Mimi, your pay and benefits comes out of the joint venture accounts same as before. Frank, I have good reason to believe I won't be worrying about money anymore. I'm doubling your pay. But I am going to need much more obstruction of justice from you. From now on, you work one-third for the Commonwealth of Virginia and two-thirds for me. And no mistakes."

"Yes, sir. And thank you," uttered the gruff-voiced detective.

"Obviously, I have to appear more in the background than ever. We meet every Sunday night. The girls and the other employees don't see me anymore. They all report to you alone, Mimi. Last thing: I'm branching out just before I go on the court. The Lounge will front for another operation I can't tell you about right now."

"I'm used to leaning on you, Jack," Mimi said. "What if I can't handle things? What if I get into trouble?"

"You won't, my dear. Just run the house like normal, and Frank and I are a phone call away. If on the off chance any investigation presents itself, the trail stops with you, Mimi. But Frank will shut down anything threatening before it materializes. And you always have a 'get out of jail free' card. But nothing must ever get back to me, understood? None of us are safe if it does."

Both Mimi and McSherry nodded in the affirmative. The detective was delighted with his newfound bonus, and Mimi was as pleased as ever to be making money doing something naughty. Devereaux was satisfied that he could trust the loyalty and competence of his partners in crime.

"Mr. Devereaux, there is one problem I need to let you in on."

"What is it, Frank?"

"Some local reporter was nosing around here earlier today trying to get in the house, posing as a customer. Of course, he didn't have the password, and I can spot reporters a mile away."

"And?" inquired Jack.

"And he's in the basement right now, handcuffed to the radiator. What do you want me to do with him?"

Jack's demeanor took a sudden sinister turn. "Give him the Eastern Kentucky treatment," he said. "I'm leaving now anyway. Until next Sunday, then."

"Yes, sir," nodded Frank.

"Bye, dreamboat. I'll be thinking about you all week," said an impassioned and frustrated Mimi.

As Jack mounted his oversized black Yukon SUV, he could faintly hear, "No, please, please," and then a scream from inside the house. He smiled. Then, the future judge drove away into the dark country night.

CHAPTER 4

In many respects, the Devereaux clan are the quintessential southern family, both in terms of sensibility and peculiarities. Do not be fooled by the southern man's reserved and quiet demeanor, though. For deep inside his soul rumbles a volcanic passion accentuating what he loves, and also what he hates. Temper all this with traditional American morality and a Roman sense of honor and the southern character presents itself without difficulty. The problem for Judge Devereaux is that he failed to inherit the ethical piece of the puzzle. Despite the rearing and teaching of his dear and saintly mother, those particular lessons never took root. Instead, he always seemed to drift through life with that rumbling volcanic passion for what he loved and hated. And he learned to conceal his emotions and cloak them with deception at a young age.

The ancient Greeks catalogued their sins, large and small, as we have in our time. Number one on their list was *hubris*, that outrageous arrogance that the rules apply to everyone except oneself. Historically, many men of hubris were so arrogant that they were incapable of grasping the fact. But our Judge was more self aware. When he thought or behaved arrogantly, it was always with his own conscious approval. And if there was one type of person he hated, it was reporters and the media. Anyone who had the audacity to stick their nose in his business, who thought they could catch Devereaux in some illicit act or outsmart him in any way, incurred his violent southern wrath!

As to the unfortunate journalist apprehended by McSherry, he was let go with a broken arm and a death threat of such believability that he moved out of state the following week. When the policeman called him early Monday morning to let him know, Devereaux just smiled the smile of the devious and hung up the phone. As he tied his tie and combed his hair, he lingered in front of the mirror and grinned: "Nobody, nobody, is ever going to get old Jack Devereaux."

As he arrived at his office, Jeri was fielding a call from the Clerk of the Fauquier Circuit Court. His swearing-in ceremony was to be at noon a week from Friday, she told him. "A week and a half of freedom," he muttered under his breath.

"How shall I occupy myself?"

If history was any guide, it would be with power games and sexual escapades. As he sat at his desk, he kept the door open so he could gawk at his secretary. Then he pulled up photos of Mimi and of several other women on his computer. He looked at them intently, and lustfully. Then he looked at Jeri. Then back at the other photos. "Son of a bitch," he whispered to himself as an inconvenient conflict emerged between two things that he loved: Geraldine and other women. Lots of other women. He thought rather torturously for a moment, then deleted the photos from his computer, sat back in his chair, and sighed. It was at that very moment that Devereaux decided that he had to marry Miss Geraldine and embrace all that came with it. He had grown to love the woman with a great intensity, which only strengthened with the passing of each day. It would also please his parents and help his career and public image to have such a wife.

Devereaux was not at all certain he could behave himself as a husband. But he was determined to try. Jeri winked at him as she returned some client calls. Jack winked back at her as he made a phone call to the fanciest jewelry store in town. Seeing no good reason to delay the action, he excused himself and walked down Main Street.

Two hours later, Jeri was still working on those party invitations as she turned around and saw her grinning boss walk in. Devereaux wasted no time getting down on one knee. "Geraldine Pike, I did not lie when I said I couldn't do without you. I can't. I love you more than I can say, and I will do my very best to make you happy every day for the rest of your life."

Jeri was floored, half-surprised and half-expecting. She cried a little when he pulled out a beautiful and classy ring of platinum sporting a three-carat, near flawless round diamond. "I'm very sorry to do this in the office of all places, but will you do me the supreme honor of being my wife?"

The answer from her was an unqualified, "Yes," and Jack locked the office door before he got back down on his knees and threw himself into Jeri's arms. Their embrace lasted many minutes. And he cried harder than she did.

* * *

Seeking his mother's approval of this welcome life change, Jack sped off toward Bourbon Hill, leaving Jeri to gush over her exceptional engagement ring and spend the next hour on the phone with her mother. As he passed through the gate and up the hill, Jack could see his father chipping golf balls onto a small makeshift green he had installed years before. "Hello, Jack. Is your golf game any good these days?"

Surprised by the pleasant greeting, Jack took the club out of his father's hand and chipped a ball an inch from the hole. "Not bad, son, not bad," said Thomas.

"I'll get right down to business, Pop. I proposed to Geraldine today, and she said yes."

"Well, a step in the right direction for sure," chimed in the father.

"So, you're pleased with the way things have been going recently?"

"Who wouldn't be? Go inside and tell your mother. I'll be in momentarily," Thomas said.

Corinne greeted the welcome news as expected. "I never thought I would be so busy at my age. I get to plan your judgeship reception, and a wedding. Jeri is able to have children, I assume?"

"I'm sure she is, but I am not exactly thrilled to have kids anytime soon," Jack said. "And she has never expressed any interest in having children to me."

"She will now that the two of you are getting married. Trust me on that one."

Devereaux just sipped his scotch and stared out the window. He had very big plans for himself, plans which took on a new dimension since his judicial appointment. Sacrifice and additional responsibility, however, were not included in those plans. But he placated his mother all the same. "Perhaps you're right. She and I ought to the have the conversation."

"Well, you will certainly possess the means to support a family," said Corrine. "And I don't mean just your judge's salary."

Jack had to stop himself from laughing wickedly at his mother's comment. He now had three income sources: a state government salary, several millions of dollars from his illegal enterprises, and if his mother maintained her wishes, one-third of an $3.5 billion inheritance. All he needed to do in the short run was put his priorities in the right place. The 64-dollar question to ask Devereaux was, why he needed to continue with his criminal schemes like The Lounge if he were financially set for life.

Since smart people who indulge in illegal commerce do it mainly for the profits, why keep yourself vulnerable if you already have enough money? This is a question that Devereaux had asked himself repeatedly and was surprisingly unable to answer. He owned Mimi's Lounge, not out of any desperation, but because he wanted to. He enjoyed the business, and he enjoyed breaking that particular law. Any reasonable person would dump the illicit activity prior to becoming a judge. Would Jack? At this point, nobody, including Jack, knew the answer.

With a special insight into the mind of our hero/anti-hero, this author thinks that Devereaux might continue to live the double-life, to play the honest judge and family man off and against the criminal mastermind, and see which persona supplied him with the most thrills and satisfaction. The icing on this particular cake would be getting away with the whole deception in the first place. A master player's hustle of Shakespearean proportion. Not just the thrill of winning, but the irresistible charm of the game itself is what seemed to captivate Jack Devereaux.

"Well," he addressed himself silently in front of his mother, "I have eight years to decide whether to play this game or find a safer and more legal one to play." In eight years, he would have to begin his campaign for reappointment by the legislature. And he was just cocky enough to believe he could get away with anything during that period.

"I have to go, Mom, but would you do something for me?"

"Certainly sweetheart!"

"I have to go to Richmond for two days of meetings. I'm leaving in the morning. Please invite Jeri to dinner and help her start planning things. She's been working feverishly on my invitations."

"Oh, sweet thing!" said Corrine. "Consider it done."

"Thanks, Mom, have a good evening."

Jack shook hands with his father on the way out to his car and got the rare slap on the back; a sign of affection in the world of the wealthy and reserved. He drove straight over to Jeri's and poured himself another drink before they sat down to a delicious Cajun meal. Jeri ate her food but never looked at it once. She could not take her eyes off Devereaux.

"Mama is so thrilled about us getting married, honey," she said. "But she told me the most curious thing."

"What was that?" Jack inquired.

"She said not to pressure you about having children. That maybe I'm too self-absorbed to be a parent." Jeri looked perplexed by the comment that she didn't see coming. Jack lightly stabbed his thigh under the table with his fork to keep from smiling, for he was elated that someone else had unwittingly begun to do his dirty work.

CHAPTER 5

No seemingly stupendous event could have been more anti-climactic than Judge Jack Devereaux's swearing-in ceremony. The Chief Judge of the Fauquier Circuit Court presided, and the whole thing was over in minutes. But that fact, which was not lost on Geraldine and Mrs. Corrine Devereaux, was less than significant to Jack. The only important matter was that he was now a judge. And for nine years to boot. The treacherous place in his brain went straight to work, imagining and plotting how his newly acquired power would stimulate his game: to boldly, cleverly dispense justice and uphold the law, and with much malice aforethought, break many a rule to serve his personal interests. And those of the game itself.

Devereaux had wanted to speed through the ceremony and go home with Jeri to spend Friday night and Saturday drunk and naked. The party in Jack's honor would be held at Bourbon Hill on Sunday afternoon—just a few lawyer friends, neighbors, and close compatriots Jack had amassed over the years. Jeri and Corrine had great fun planning the event, and predictably Jeri inquired of the new judge what he had been doing in Richmond earlier that week. "Meeting with the legislators that offered me this position. You know, and getting them drunk, strip clubs and all," Jack teased.

"Ha-ha, Judge Devereaux. You better plan on flying right from now on," said a playful Geraldine.

Of course, the naked truth was that Devereaux didn't meet with anyone in Richmond except the superintendent of the State Police. The meeting had one simple goal: to convince the chief that he should assign Detective Sergeant Frank McSherry as Judge Devereaux's personal bodyguard. "I know I have a bailiff and security men at the courthouse in Warrenton," claimed Jack. "But I will be handling the most serious felony cases in the circuit, and my family is rich. And everyone knows it. You'd be doing my family and I a big favor, Chief. One that I'm sure to remember for quite a long time! Are we on the same page?"

The superintendent leaned back in his chair, smiled at Devereaux, then robustly leapt to his feet as the two men shook hands. "I'll put the order in tomorrow, Judge. McSherry is yours."

Obviously, Judge Devereaux could have had the detective resign and be his chief of security privately. But that would miss the point entirely. McSherry was to be of a combined use to the judge—security, and a partner in crime within the state law enforcement community. As Devereaux and Jeri bid his parents goodbye until Sunday, they rushed to his car intent on burning rubber and arrive at Jeri's house as soon as they could get inside, undress, and make the old wood floors shake for a few hours. The couple entered the car, and both checked their phones and messages.

Jeri sat and texted back and forth with her mother as Jack looked angrily at the mountain of messages Mimi had left him. "Jack. I need you, Jack, tonight."

The lewdness of these particular messages made even Jack turn red. "Damn her antics," said Jack under his breath. He knew he had only himself to blame. He had corrupted an otherwise sweet and good-natured young woman several years ago. Because of Devereaux, a young real estate agent who worked for her mother had been seduced into a life of licentious and carnal activity. You could say that Devereaux showed a degree of decency when he made Mimi the Madame, encouraging her not to sell herself but to remain his constant plaything. Nonetheless, the damage was complete with poor Mimi addicted to Devereaux's charms and attention and up to her nose in a criminal enterprise.

Knowing that he could not ignore her all weekend, Jack got out of his car and dialed her. "My folks have me tied up through Sunday. I will call Frank and change the meeting to Monday night. Much will be revealed."

"I can't wait that long, Jack. Please come and see me," begged Mimi.

"Monday at 4 p.m. Make sure you're alone, okay?"

"Okay, Mr.—Oops. I mean *Judge* Devereaux, you stud."

"Bye, Mimi. And no more text messages. Only calls."

Devereaux, shocked that he got off so easily, reentered his car and leaned over to Jeri for a kiss.

"All of your wheeling and dealing done for the day, mystery man?" she asked.

"As a matter of fact, yes. You can enjoy two days of a reasonably transparent man, Miss Geraldine."

She winked, and he sped off to the town of Warrenton.

A few minutes later, they arrived at Jeri's old Victorian house she was renting. It had a magnificent wraparound porch and was wide and deep, painted in a beautiful Williamsburg Blue. Jeri ran upstairs to the shower and Devereaux poured himself a drink and went out to the porch swing to make a phone call. It was a picturesque day of 72 degrees with not a cloud in the sky. The drink and the swing instantly relaxed Jack from the business at hand.

"Frank, something has to be done about Mimi. She's getting worse, a real liability. No, nothing immediately. Stand down for the weekend, and meet me at The Lounge at 2 p.m. on Monday. We have to nip this in the bud." Jack casually saluted his new head of security, who drove by the house just after the phone call ended. No matter where Judge Devereaux was at the time, you could be certain that Sergeant McSherry was close by.

"What are you going to do with the office, now that you're a judge with chambers?" Jeri inquired as she descended the stairs to the living room.

"It's an office condo, which I own. I guess I will sell it. Why? Do you want it?"

"I like going to that office. It's like a second home," she sighed.

"Then you will have it. I've got several mortgage payments left. Then I will title it over to us both. Speaking of homes, Jeri," Jack said as he moved into Jeri's spread-out arms, "I have something for you, in your top kitchen drawer."

Geraldine's face suddenly took on a little-girl-on-Christmas-morning look. It was quite endearing and very fetching to Jack, who sat down and sipped his scotch, watching his eager playmate. She pulled out a deed paper giving her full title to the house she was renting, and secretly coveted. "Are you kidding me, lover? This is for real?"

"Absolutely, my dear."

"But why aren't you on the deed with me, sweetheart?" she asked.

"Mainly for tax reasons, honey. I will explain when we start filing after the New Year."

"Judge Devereaux, I am going to rock your privileged little world in about 10 minutes," said Jeri with such a teasing seductiveness that Devereaux had to cross his legs and grab himself. As she bent over in front of him to pick up the paper she had dropped in all her giddiness, the judge threw down the last of his drink and chased Jeri upstairs. She performed on him as promised and sweetened all of the complex and hedonistic plans he had in store for them that evening.

Jeri knew she was a world-class beauty and that men in general lusted after her. But weighing in at 180 pounds made her self-conscious. Never mind that she was five-foot-nine and had excellent muscle tone and a perfectly curved figure. She was especially conscious of her butt, where she could put on weight quite easily. Devereaux was the opposite. He loved Jeri's butt and thunder thighs so much that he nearly lost his senses; and that was when she was clothed. Naked and hot, Geraldine transported Devereaux into a moaning, panting lap dog. And the fatter she got below the waist only heightened the senses. After several climaxes, he kissed her and lay on top of her, hugging her tightly. Jeri hugged him back, and they lay that way for a long while. They didn't talk much, and they both knew they were loved.

Monday afternoon came soon enough. Jack and McSherry met at The Lounge at 2 p.m. The detective grabbed a cold six pack of Budweiser and drank it impressively fast. It was warm outside, so Devereaux stuck with fruit juice. "I'm closing The Lounge, *el permanente*," said Devereaux.

"What about Mimi and the girls?" inquired McSherry.

"The girls will stay in my employ. They've earned it, and I'm working on the best way to use their considerable talents," said Jack.

"And our Madame?" McSherry asked.

"Mimi has to be pacified. She's a threat to my impending marriage. And a threat to my marriage is also a threat to my fortune."

"What do you propose to do, Judge?"

"Do you want her? As your squeeze, I mean. I see you how you look at her, Frank."

McSherry looked annoyed and titillated at the same time. "What are you getting at?" he asked.

"If she was your girlfriend, you would enjoy pleasures most men only dream of. And she would remain very easily controlled. A win-win for everyone."

"Yeah, except I don't know if she even likes me," Frank said.

"Sure, she does. She thinks you're a fine-looking man and a real strong protector. She told me herself."

"I'm not much with words, Judge; especially when it comes to women."

"Allow me to fix this up right. She'll do anything I suggest. Then, at least for the moment, she won't give us anything to be worried about. Her biggest problem is drinking, then her mouth, after she's had too much. Do this for me, will you, Frank? I would be mighty grateful," Devereaux said as he put a hand on Frank's shoulder.

"If you can convince her to be with me, I'm all in. The way she powders that butt of hers..."

"I know, makes you sweat bullets, doesn't it?" Jack exclaimed. "Leave it to me, Frank, and by the end of the week she will be as constant a companion as you desire. And very willing. When she hasn't had too much to drink, she really has quite a pleasing and yielding disposition."

McSherry's usual stoic demeanor gave way to a happy anticipation, one he had not felt in some time. He was grateful to Devereaux, and Devereaux knew it.

Mimi showed up just after 3 p.m., and the group had an intense discussion about the future of their impending escapade. "Good afternoon, Mimi," Devereaux said as he softly kissed her on the lips. "I see no reason to delay, so grab a drink and allow me to share a piece of my vision with you."

"To begin, I have rethought the matter and have decided that I cannot be a Circuit Judge and own a house of prostitution. The potential for error and unwanted publicity is too great. Frank, thankfully you were on your toes the other week when that snot-nosed reporter came sniffing around. But we may not be so lucky the next time. Therefore, as of right now, The Lounge is no more. The girls, as I told Frank, are still on my payroll. Not one of you have to worry about pay and health insurance. However! Mimi, I suggest you go back to your mom and sell real estate for a while, until I put the finish on our new operation."

As usual, Mimi's curiosity exploded into the conversation. "What new business? Tell me! Please tell me, Jack," she said as she cuddled up next to him, swiping her hips on his waist.

An irritated but gentile Devereaux seated her back down at the table. "Today is strictly business," he said. McSherry could think of little else than that it would soon be him who Miss Mimi would be cuddling. "I know I told you both that details on this would be forthcoming at today's sit-down. Call me superstitious, but I'm going to wait until the entire idea is in place. Give me two more weeks."

"I want to make Jack a special drink to celebrate his becoming a judge, and also for crafting what I just know will be a delicious way to make money," Mimi said as she went behind the bar, rummaged around, and came out with a savory drink. "Here you are, Mr. Judge Devereaux, a very dirty martini!" Mimi grinned lustfully as she handed the drink to Devereaux. The judge and the detective laughed. All the room was relaxed at that moment.

Both Mimi and Frank knew they were secure, as well as the working girls with whom Jack would meet separately. Frank had his police job and salary and was getting big bonuses from Devereaux as his head of security. That arrangement technically violated state law, but oh well!

Mimi was less well-versed in the ways of the world, but Jack had always taken care of her, so she entertained no worries on that score. The three cohorts just enjoyed more drink and idle conversation, and Mimi and McSherry would be in for the surprise of their lives two weeks hence, when Judge Devereaux would serve up the most wickedly ingenious plot that could ever satiate their scheming and entitled designs.

CHAPTER 6

"All rise! Court is now in session; the Honorable John P. Devereaux presiding," declared the Fauquier County Deputy Sheriff.

In the Commonwealth of Virginia, court begins theoretically at 9 a.m. In actuality, it begins whenever the judge arrives in the courtroom. Judge Devereaux decided to keep everyone in suspense his first day on the bench and arrived at 9:30 a.m. He had been on the lawyer side of things for quite a while, lingering in waiting for the presence of judges and licking their boots when he had to. Now it was time for his boots to be licked, and he was enjoying it thoroughly. He had decided upon a strategy of being the gentleman judge of the circuit. Gentility and politeness would be offered to the vast majority of attorneys and litigants, witnesses, and defendants. This way, he could amass eight years of good will in the legal community and secure his reappointment when the time came. The strategy also allowed for him to be high-handed and wrathful toward those who pissed him off.

His first two weeks on the job would be anti-climatic and quite a bore—motions filed, appeals from lawyers in cases with clients from the lower courts involving mostly petty matters. "The most routine of routine business conceivable," Devereaux told Jeri on the Friday after his second week had finished.

"If it's this lame, why would you want the job?" she interjected.

The judge scooted over to Jeri's side of the living room sofa and rested his fingers gently on her chin. "Power and pleasing my parents are attractive enough to me to do many jobs I would not ordinarily do. But despite the less than thrilling start, I believe this appointment will be a gift that keeps on giving. You'll see."

"I think you get off on people calling you *Judge*," said a sly Geraldine.

"Careful. You may offend the dignity of my court," Devereaux teased. "I am a judge on and off the bench, remember that."

"I am ever so sorry, Judge Devereaux! What, pray tell, is my punishment to be?"

Devereaux winked at her as he chugged his wine. "Your ass is mine!" he declared as Jeri screamed and laughed, running upstairs with the judge closing in behind her.

If any passersby had happened outside the house in the next hour, they might faintly have heard a high-pitched, sexy woman's voice providing the icing on the cake: "Oh my, Judge, you are the handsomest, hottest, most powerful man who ever lived!"

It was times like those that the judge really enjoyed being himself. He knew Jeri was good at the fantasy games. He also knew his fiancée thought he hung the moon. Hence, the heightened state of the fantastical encounters. They were based upon real and deep feelings, from both of them. There would be much pleasure that weekend, which was good for the judge. He would need a clear head on Monday evening when he got down to business with Mimi and McSherry. What he would manage to pull off would make his friends rich and solidify Devereaux as a player among players, the successful judge, and the successful scofflaw. An heir to a fortune and life with the woman of his dreams and obsession.

But would there be a price to pay for this bounty of good fortune?

Sunday afternoon and evening was spent at Bourbon Hill. It was the first full family dinner since Jack and Geraldine had gotten engaged and he had become a judge. It was a family in the biological sense, but an odder collection of characters could hardly be imagined. For starters, Jack's two sisters could not have been more different. Mary Jane Devereaux was old-school charm like her mother, single, and a successful therapist and professor of psychiatry at the University of Virginia. She was only 42 years old. Mary Jane was adopted when the elder Devereauxs were told they couldn't have children.

But seven years later, Corrine bore Jack, and then Courtney afterwards. Lovely, poised, and accomplished, one could imagine her the favored child of both parents. But dysfunctional wealthy southern families don't work that way. She was the favorite of neither mom nor dad, hence the deeply rooted complex she carried with her, along with her successes. No, Judge Jack was indisputably his mother's favorite child, who despite his dubious character could do no wrong in Corrine Devereaux's eyes.

The favorite child of Mr. Thomas Devereaux was the baby of the family, 28-year-old Courtney Mansfield, wife of Timothy Mansfield of the wealthy and illustrious Albemarle County Mansfields. The pair had met at the University of Richmond, Tim falling in love at first sight, and Courtney leading him on and torturing him with half-assed affection until she decided it was time to settle down with someone at least as rich as her parents. And someone she could lead around like a puppy dog for the rest of their lives.

Hate is a strong word that is thrown around too loosely. But it would be no exaggeration to say that Courtney and Jack hated each other's guts. Not usually prone to pity or excessive compassion, Devereaux felt genuinely sorry for his brother-in-law. Courtney never missed an opportunity to drink too much at these family gatherings and eventually embarrass and degrade her husband in front of everyone. Humiliation never seemed too far away for poor Timothy at such events, and Jack would waste no time coming to his rescue, always at the expense of his younger sister. Predictably, Corrine would politely side with Jack, Thomas with Courtney, and all at the grotesque discomfort of Mary Jane.

Thus, the oldest and most respectable Devereaux child would be treated like the stepchild, and neither parent could ever seem to muster the psychological insight to understand what they were doing to Mary Jane. They simply were clueless that they unconsciously loved their adopted child slightly less than their biological ones. Which explains the special relationship between her and Jack. One might not be too extreme in speculating that Mary Jane would find an excuse every time not to go to one of her parents' dinners, but for the presence of her brother. So, this admirable lady adored Jack every bit as much as their mother, albeit for entirely different reasons.

While Corrine thought her son the most thoroughly excellent child who ever existed, Mary Jane loved her brother chiefly in a reciprocal fashion, for his tangible affection and defense of her honor in a silly and often cruel family environment. Mary Jane Devereaux was under her brother's spell and would do nearly anything for him.

Timothy Mansfield faced a similar emotional predicament, with his frivolous and uncaring wife coupled with a lordly father-in-law ready to cut off any man's head who had a cross word to say about Courtney. Since Jack was entirely unafraid of his father, he would let Courtney have it right between the eyes whenever and however it pleased him. Thus, Timothy was under Jack's spell and would quietly do his bidding whenever asked.

If these familial diplomatic skills could transcend the social climate at Bourbon Hill, Devereaux shouldn't need a criminal scheme to satisfy him. He could soar in the legal and political world. But, alas for our judge, the wider world offered up too many rules and eggs to break. The temptation was inescapable. So, our vain and corrupt judge, villain though he be, was most assuredly the hero to two very sensitive and insecure personages. Throw in Geraldine Pike, who wept compassion for any victim of cruelty, always looking for an excuse to support her fiancé, and you had a powder keg charged and lit by Sunday afternoon when all parties arrived at

Bourbon Hill within minutes of each other.

Judge Devereaux gave his chief of security the night off. He was, after all, at his parents' estate, which was patrolled by sheriff's deputies moonlighting as security personnel. Detective McSherry was enjoying his Sunday over at Mimi's place. Thanks to Devereaux's instructions, Mimi had talked herself into a relationship with Frank. McSherry was on a cloud-nine high, drinking with and making love to the sexiest woman he could imagine. The two spoke endlessly over what Jack had in mind for them the coming Monday night. They speculated, but neither of them could make any educated guess as to what would replace Mimi's Lounge. They were content to wait, for Devereaux had never disappointed or bored them in the past.

Sunday cocktail hour at Bourbon Hill commenced promptly at 4 p.m. Mary Jane politely kissed her parents and escaped to the wet bar off the main parlor, knowing well ahead of time that cosmopolitans would be, along with her brother, the only tonic to get her through the night. The judge and Geraldine walked in very soon after his sister. Mary Jane threw down the first of many drinks and literally sprinted over to the couple, hugging Jeri tightly, as though she had just discovered a sister who was actually human. She gave her brother the same treatment, smearing lipstick all over his face. Jack's presence softened his mother even further. Jeri's presence pacified his father.

Could it be that the society of the Devereaux was being transported to something altogether gentler? It seemed for 20 minutes or so that all was right with the world at Bourbon Hill. Love, respect, and genuine familial affirmation permeated the atmosphere of the grand estate. Five people were enjoying each other's company, drinking, and conversing amiably, like normal people. Like a family.

Then, the bitch of the ball arrived!

Courtney and her luckless husband made their greetings. Thomas, as usual, was overjoyed at seeing his prize child. Contrasting the two Devereaux sisters was easy. Mary Jane was tall and athletic with an elegant and pretty face; she was quite ladylike and reserved. Courtney was the life of the party, vivacious and petite. She also sported a very pretty face but in the more endearingly cute variety. From an early age, whenever her parents presented her anywhere in society her cheeks were always pinched, accompanied by a sigh from people: "Oh, how precious! What a simply precious and pretty young lady." Courtney could put her eyes and smile to work and charm a squirrel right out of a tree.

She was sufficiently younger than Mary Jane, so a conventional sibling rivalry did not exist between the two. But the older sister grew to be appalled at the younger's disingenuous and shamefully self-serving behavior toward the family and people in general. One would think that Jack would resent having a rival in his family for self-serving manipulation, but the younger sister was a piker compared to Jack. Courtney's methods of always getting her way were obvious and overbearing, while Jack's were wickedly subtle. The judge's intellect and operational prowess dwarfed that of his silly sibling. The icing on the cake for Jack that evening was to have Courtney's entrance and the fawning on of her father overshadowed by Geraldine's beauty and warmth.

The impending wife of Judge Devereaux walked across the large parlor room and kissed Courtney. "Don't you look lovely tonight, Mrs. Mansfield," she stated. "And Mr. Mansfield, I don't recall you being this handsome, especially in your tuxedo. Courtney, you've got a real catch," Jeri said as she gently hugged Timothy.

Tactless to the last, Courtney just sauntered off to the bar, waving her hand. "Whatever!" said the little brat.

Jeri returned to her seat on the sofa next to her fiancé, whispering in his ear, "You can slice the tension in this room with a knife. When is dinner being served?"

"Relax and just be your charming self, honey. It's going to be a long evening. Leave my sister to me!"

Nothing but trivial conversation accompanied dinner. Jack ate the food, with extra bread and large portions. He knew that he needed a very full stomach for the amount of alcohol he had consumed and was to consume later. Jack was one of those types who knew how to drink heavily and stop before his faculties became entirely impaired. Drinking enhanced his sharp tongue and his wit to back it up. Nobody relished a verbal confrontation with this man. When he was riled, he could make his opponent suffer like few people could. A long stare and an evil grin were followed by a rhetorical flourish of elevated knowledge and biting sarcasm, reducing any unfortunate antagonist to frustration and defeat. These qualities would prove to make Judge Devereaux invincible in the courtroom.

Jeri knew all of this about her man, and when she was advised to "leave my sister to me," she felt sorry for Courtney. One could imagine what might be in store for the hapless young Devereaux sister, were she to say anything which might serve her up as cannon fodder for Jack.

Fortunately for the sake of superior family drama, she did.

Meanwhile, just a few miles away, Detective Frank McSherry took a break from his impassioned week with Mimi to perform a task for the judge. He called his brother and three of his cousins in Pike County, Kentucky. The men were all former specialists in the Army—the cousins working the sprawling family farm which grew, raised, and grazed a multitude of crops and livestock, and his brother Brian, the Sheriff of Buchanan County, Virginia, just over the state line. These individuals were to comprise a small special operations group of muscle and covert activities for the new organization the judge was piecing together. These were formidable men in any circle or circumstance. Pike County, incidentally, is legendary for the most famous family feud in American history: the Hatfields and the McCoys. Many McCoy descendants still reside in that part of Kentucky. The Hatfields lived and operated in the southeastern corner of West Virginia.

It is difficult to explain just how tough and brutally efficient in all forms of fighting and killing the Scots Irish men of Appalachia are and have always been. In the 18th Century, they defeated formidable Native American tribes, beating them at their own game of mountain guerrilla tactics. They shot at and chased out of the hills many Confederate Army units because they were too independent minded to join the Civil War conflict. Those who did join units in either the Union or Confederate armies proved to be the best soldiers in the war. McSherry and his kinfolk grew up hunting and tracking. They were poor but had farms, went to church, and were instilled with kindly values. A McSherry would give you the shirt off his back if you were a friend in need. A stranger might receive similar kindness.

But heaven help those who would dare to tread on that family. The boys were as strong as oxen and could fight like badgers. At a young age, they were all crack shots with handguns, shotguns, and rifles. Seldom did any of them ever miss a target, not at any range. There is a good reason why organized crime families and gangs never settled in southern Appalachia; they wouldn't survive a week! The Mafia, drug gangs, nor criminal scumbags from the city were even close to a match for these country boys. One wrong move from any outsider in these hills ended in a particular result—his getting hung from the tallest tree in the county.

Thus, whatever our judge was cooking up, he would have as tough and competent a Praetorian Guard as possible—one unquestionably loyal to Frank McSherry, and to Judge Devereaux by default. "I knew I could count on you and the fellows Brian. We're all going to make a bundle of money," Frank said. Then he and his brother exchanged a family joke and hung up their phones.

Back at Bourbon Hill, Judge Devereaux was seated between Jeri and his older sister, Mary Jane. All throughout the dinner, he paid extra close attention to Mary Jane, who needed to feel some love. Jeri's job was to keep the parents charmed and play "good cop" to Jack's "bad cop" when relating to Courtney, who made the mistake of questioning Jack's credentials to be a judge in the first place. Positively inebriated, Jack fired a salvo after Corrine and Thomas gently ordered the children out onto the veranda. "Seen any good polo matches lately, Courtney?"

Timothy turned beet red while Courtney just gave the judge a stare. It was a stare that said, "I wish I had the guts and the strength to beat you to death right here, right now." Geraldine stood her ground, giving Courtney and her mortified husband a wink, and then sat Jack down, saying, "I think we could use a good polo match to go to together, huh, Jack?" Jeri didn't know it, but she really had stepped in a puddle.

Jack started laughing uncontrollably. "I love you to pieces, Jeri. You are so earnest," he said. Courtney rushed inside to the powder room with Timothy following behind. Jack then fixed another drink and explained to his fiancée that one summer when Courtney was on break from college, she and her friends were crazy obsessed with some of the players on the local polo team. Through the brother of one the friends, Jack heard that his sister had serviced at least three of the players in the stables one night.

When he confronted Courtney, she never bothered to deny the rumor. He explained to Jeri that although some might accuse him of ramp hypocrisy, he lost what little respect he had for his younger sister at that point. Jeri neither wanted to excuse or condemn her sister-in-law-to-be. She simply put her arms around Jack and asked him if he could at least be civil for the rest of the evening. The judge complied, knowing his lady's suggestion could easily morph into an order. For a man used to getting his way with other people, he was surprisingly malleable when it came to Geraldine. She was the person he felt most compelled to please. Realizing this fact from the beginning of their relationship he endeavored to conceal from her a large and looming piece of his character. For her own good, as well as for his, under no circumstances could she be privy to his dark dealings.

Monday evening came round quickly enough. Devereaux dropped a bomb in his meeting with Frank McSherry and Mimi. His master plan was two-pronged: secure his position of power in the Commonwealth of Virginia and destroy his sister, Courtney, in the eyes of their parents, leaving himself and his sister Mary Jane to divide the family fortune. Some background into Jack's thinking is necessary to this plan. When his Senator client first suggested he accept the position of Circuit Judge, he did his homework on the powers that be in the legislature. What he found was that his state was divided down the middle between Republicans and Democrats, each party not having quite enough power to guarantee a stable government in excess of four years. This volatility offended the ambitions of Jack Devereaux, for he had long term plans for himself and his lady. There was simply no way to predict who would be in power in the General Assembly in nine years. No matter who he courted and how successfully he maneuvered himself, there was an equal chance some other group of people would be in charge of appointing judges.

He was also certain that his father would look upon any failure to be reappointed as catastrophic, and the old man would instantly turn against his son. Such a contingency was unacceptable to Jack. The Senate Leader and the Speaker of the House of Delegates who rammed through his appointment should be receptive to reappointment, but nine years is a lifetime in politics. The men might no longer be in their offices then. Devereaux might make some judicial decisions which would make him fall out of favor with certain key legislators. The judge had decided from the beginning that his career and access to his inheritance must absolutely not depend on the political maneuvering of others. Anything less than a guaranteed reappointment was out of the question.

But for a guarantee, Devereaux needed insurance. Hence, the lovely ladies from The Lounge. And of course, Sergeant Frank McSherry and the boys from Kentucky.

"I knew there was a good reason for all those hidden cameras in the rooms," exclaimed an emboldened Mimi as she suddenly deduced that the house of ill repute had also been a blackmailing operation from the very beginning. McSherry had known, for he had the cameras installed himself.

"My dear friends," said Devereaux. "There are politicians, businessmen, lawyers, and police officers on these tapes going back to when we opened up The Lounge four years ago. There is enough dirt for us to court favors and payoffs for years. But not enough to get me what I desire."

"What's that, dreamboat?" Mimi asked.

Devereaux tossed back his scotch and placed his hand on McSherry's shoulder. He then put his empty glass down and kissed Mimi on both cheeks. "We are going to go 'scorched earth' on Virginia politicians. In eight years' time, we will have dirt, filth, and leverage on everyone we need down at the Capitol."

"How do we pull this one off, Judge? Seems like a tall order, even for you?" inquired the sergeant.

"Have faith, Frank, have faith. I've been in tight spots before. You're going to run the girls. This time, however, it will be a mobile and more secretive operation instead of a house. The finest ladies of the evening Virginia has ever seen. And available only to the most influential men in the state."

"How will my brother and cousins fit into this plan?" asked a puzzled McSherry.

"Don't you worry a bit, Frank. I have big plans for them. Let's get cranking right away on our new insurance policy. Buy the girls some new and expensive clothes and shoes. The best perfume. Tell them exactly what they're about to do and how much more money they're going to make. I need senators and delegates in my pocket starting right about now!"

The beauty and overpowering sex appeal of Devereaux's women would rival any ancient harem. Any middle-aged man would be easy prey for these girls. But politicians, it has been said, are unusually horny, so the seasoned power brokers in Jack's crosshairs would not stand a chance.

After the Judge outlined another part of the plan, McSherry, who was not easily impressed, looked upon Devereaux with ever more esteem. To this veteran rough and tumble cop, the young judge was proving to be the ultimate boss who had his undying loyalty and respect. A wealthy patrician who could inspire and lead others in his schemes. A superior criminal mastermind on one level, perhaps. No matter how you define it, Frank McSherry and his brother and cousins were ready to serve this man, and with few—if any—ethical limitations. The only thing left was to launch operation ruin upon his younger sister, Courtney, for Jack had big plans for her as well.

CHAPTER 7

The next day, Devereaux walked into his office and bid good morning to his legal secretary and clerks. It was to be a slow week with no trials. Just motions, docket case rotations and the judges' personal favorite: sentencing. Devereaux wanted to establish a fast reputation as a hanging judge toward bad people who do bad things, and as a fountain of mercy toward defendants who were basically good people who had made unfortunate mistakes. As he entered his chambers, he noticed Detective McSherry removing some cameras.

"I thought I had those removed on the first day," said an irate Judge Devereaux.

"The Chief Judge says he wants cameras in all offices and chambers."

"The office is fine, but not in here. You tell him...never mind," said the judge as he picked up his phone. "Fred, this is Jack Devereaux. Fine, fine. I'm getting situated quite well, thank you. I'm sending these cameras back to administration. I have a Chief of Security, and I don't want any audio-visual devices in my private chambers." The voice on the other line was noticeably raised. "I have no problem following courthouse procedures and regulations. You're doing a fine job," said Jack. "But no cameras or any other electronic bullshit in here. A judge has to have some privacy, for piss sakes! All right, I figured you'd see my point. Thank you, Fred."

McSherry looked at Devereaux with a slight grin. Apparently, his boss was so smooth he could dictate to the chief of the circuit court. "Won't your pressing the matter raise suspicion to the rest of the judges? Like you have something to hide," McSherry exclaimed.

"Perhaps, but you and I are going to be having conversations; conversations between us and with other people. I can't have any of that on record," said a confident Devereaux. "Are all the devices disabled, Frank?"

"Yes, sir, they are."

"Okay, down to business. Those Central Americans in jail for Fentanyl dealing, who are they?"

"There are four altogether; two have those gang tattoos and the others look like underlings," said Frank. "Do they have the money, or did it exchange hands already?"

"My state boys got the dope, and the defense lawyer said they can lead us to the money if they are released. They say about $420,000. Since they were dealing with another group, they have no loyalty, so they will tell us where to find the others. I'm not sure I'd trust them with that."

Devereaux pulled out a sheet of paper and signed it. "Go down to the jail and show this to the deputy in charge. It's a release order via their cooperation. Have them take you to the money. Are our friends from Kentucky operational?"

"Yes, they are, Judge," Frank nodded.

"Good. Have them follow you, and when you get to the money, it's the backwoods treatment for them, understood?"

"The boys will be glad to apply it, sir."

"If they don't know where the cash is after all, same treatment applies," barked a commanding Devereaux. "I hate foreigners who come into my county and commit crimes; it's considerably more offensive than locals doing it."

"I hear you, Judge! We don't like them either!"

"Off to the races then," ordered the judge. "And call me as soon as it's done."

The luckless criminals were giddy in their entirely false sense of security as McSherry led them out in handcuffs and placed them in a black Chevrolet Suburban. Frank pulled out of the station slowly and texted his three cousins, who were in a gray pickup truck. They drove for 40 minutes or so, and the lead gang member, speaking broken English, led McSherry down a gravel path into the woods. Shortly, a burned-out barn appeared, and Frank parked and let the gangsters out to retrieve the cash. The four handcuffed men identified a floorboard, and McSherry pulled out from under it a duffel bag appearing to have several hundred thousand dollars in it. The criminals were dumbly elated when McSherry unlocked their handcuffs. Frank walked out of the barn back to his vehicle. The first of the gangsters stepped slowly out of the barn and to his horror was shot in the kneecap by one of Frank's cousins. The Kentuckians stormed the premises and shot-gunned the others in their legs. Screaming and sobbing, the gangsters pleaded for their lives, but to no avail.

The McSherry cousins went to work on them with their Bowie knives, and the horrifying cries that nobody else could hear lasted just a few minutes. When the boys from Kentucky exited the barn, they had names of regional gang leaders and their whereabouts. Frank nodded approvingly at his clan members and went back inside. All that was left were four young men with their torsos slit from navel to throat and their severed thumbs and fingers stuffed in their mouths.

Before you deem to feel empathy for these unfortunate men, realize that they were suspects in several gruesome rapes and murders in the Washington, D.C., region. One of their victims was only 15 years old. These gang bangers were the worst of the worst. And Judge Devereaux was determined to make such people wish they had never even heard of Virginia, let alone set up shop there. Weeks passed and more gang members disappeared from custody, never to be seen or heard from again. Judge Devereaux purchased a farm just a few miles west of the Bourbon Hill estate. It was on high ground and wooded, with a large five-bedroom house. The Kentucky boys were living large there, undetected and undisturbed. And they were close by whenever the judge needed them. Frank McSherry kept his rented farmhouse but spent most nights with Mimi, who lived in Middleburg, the capital town of Virginia Hunt Country, and 10 miles from the defunct Upperville's Lounge.

Except for the occasional drug gang and human trafficking violence (these foreign gangs were careful to only kill or terrorize each other) most of the crime in Devereaux's circuit was theft, domestic issues, and white-collar business crimes. As previously stated, Judge Devereaux was never hesitant to show mercy to the penitent and vulnerable. After the Sheriff's men rounded up a shoplifting ring consisting mainly of poor kids, he gave all of the young-sters probation and community service due to the fact that they didn't hurt anyone. The ringleader was not so fortunate. A career criminal, he ran the little group of pickpockets like Fagin from *Oliver Twist*.

When the prosecution showed that he threatened the boys with violence to themselves and their families, Devereaux sentenced the man to life in prison, no possibility of parole. So outraged was the judge that he carried that particular case with him for many weeks. As he and McSherry left the courtroom after sentencing, they were alone in the judge's chambers.

"Make sure he goes directly to Jarrat. Not some cozy waiting room," said Devereaux. Jarrat was the name of the main Virginia state penitentiary. "Our current Governor is a little too liberal minded for my sensibilities, Frank. I'm beginning to be able to read a lawyer like a book, and I believe this fel-low's attorney is heading straight for the Governor's staff for a commutation of sentence."

"What would that mean?" asked Frank.

"It means he would be a free man in 10 years or less. And that would be quite impossible for me to tolerate," the irate judge barked.

"I know how you feel, Judge. All those kids corrupted. I could kill that man as soon as look at him," said a frightening Frank McSherry.

"We need to wait for the appeals to exhaust, courts and executive. If his sentence stands, all is well and good. But if his sentence is to be commuted..." The judge swung his chair over towards McSherry, who looked as eager as ever to receive a dark and sinister order. "Use your prison connections to see that some grave physical misfortune befalls him."

"My pleasure, sir."

On another front, the younger Devereaux sister, Mrs. Courtney Mansfield, was making her brother's plan considerably easy. Her husband was off to New England for a fraternity reunion, which she did not care to attend. Instead, she drove over to Great Meadow and caught the youngest member of her favorite polo team bailing hay.

"Hi there! It sure is a hot day, darling. Do you want to cool off with a ride?" Courtney had her Mercedes Convertible coupe, and the young man with hormones blazing hopped into the car. Courtney opened a jug full of frozen whiskey sour, and the two chugged it as Courtney sped off down the rural state highway. She was on a high. All by herself at home, plenty of money, and a naughty little afternoon with someone who tickled her fancy. She sipped more of the whiskey sour and gave some to her friend. As he drank, she squeezed his hand and tickled his left knee. The young man was all nerves, amorous and terrified at the same time. He was calmed only by Courtney's reassuring glances that suggested he was about to enjoy a day he had only ever dreamed about.

After about 20 minutes of driving, Courtney was stunned to see the red and blue flashing lights behind her. As she pulled over, she tried sliding the whiskey jug behind the driver's seat. It wouldn't fit. Just as she told her friend to keep quiet, the state trooper was upon the passenger.

"Get out of the car," he said to the polo player. The trooper handcuffed the young man and locked him in the back seat of the squad car. Courtney was now sweating and shaking, knowing that she could do nothing about the smell of alcohol leaking from her body and breath.

Pleading with the officer not to place her under arrest, she acquiesced immediately to his suggestion that she call her father and have him pick her up at the very spot where they were. She did as instructed, and Thomas Devereaux was incensed as he hung up the phone and got into his car. He sped off down the long driveway without telling his wife where he was going.

Courtney, feeling momentary relief that she would avoid arrest and a night in jail, suddenly sobered up enough to realize that the state trooper was not going anywhere. And neither was her playmate or the impounded jug of whiskey. No, her father would shortly arrive on the scene and be witness to all of her sordid behavior of the day. Nervousness gave way to panic, and she began to cry as she sat down in her car.

Meanwhile, the trooper had been slyly taking pictures of the car, the whiskey, and the two intended love birds ever since he had stopped them. He motioned for Courtney to join her friend in the squad car. As the two terrified individuals tried to console each other, the trooper poured some bourbon from a concealed flask under the seats of the car. When Thomas arrived, the stench would be unmistakable.

"Thank you, Officer, for not impounding the car and for releasing my daughter," he said.

"Well, sir, I know your family well. You're respected and upstanding citizens. What do you want me to do with the young man in my car?" asked the trooper as he showed some pictures to Thomas.

Old Mr. Devereaux snarled at his daughter. He looked at the photos again, then he snarled again at Courtney, "Do with him whatever you wish, Officer. I can assure you he is no concern of mine."

The officer left and Thomas waited for the tow truck to take Courtney's car to Bourbon Hill. He said nothing to his daughter except that she had very nearly disgraced herself and her family. The incident alone was not sufficient to disinherit her, but the die that Judge Devereaux advanced had been cast. The seed was now permanently fixed in Thomas Devereaux's unconscious mind that his son may have been right along about his favored younger daughter. All that was required was for Thomas to admit it to himself consciously, and the judge would be there at the right time to heap some more misery upon this father and daughter relationship.

Of course, the judge was thrilled with the report he received from Frank McSherry that evening. Finishing his evening patrol around their neighborhood, Jack and Geraldine invited him to dinner. After they ate, the two men sat on the porch as Geraldine cleaned up. McSherry added to Devereaux's pleasure for the day by informing him that the young polo player with his sister and several other men who worked at Great Meadow were in the country illegally. Frank called a friend of his from ICE, and the immigration authorities arrested the men and scheduled them for deportation. "You know, Frank, we basically live in a foul and rotten world, with little reason for hope, and all that shit! But when things go our way, life can really be a beautiful thing."

"I hear you, Judge," Frank said.

"You know, Frank, you're not my hired hand. I consider you a friend of the highest order. Why don't you just call me Jack, in private." McSherry was visibly overwhelmed by the gesture of friendship. "But be sure to call Jeri 'Mrs. Devereaux' when the time comes. It makes her feel important and respected."

"Sure thing...Jack," Frank said hesitantly. What a victory the two men enjoyed. The icing on the cake was that they had their victory against the powers that be in the state capital. The current Governor had directed the state police not to inform ICE every time they arrested an illegal alien. Technically, McSherry worked for the State Police Superintendent, appointed by the Governor. But all the executive powers and resources brought to bear could not penetrate our band of exceptional scofflaws. Judge Devereaux had contempt for any newfangled ideas on crime fighting. He was squarely from the old school and would undermine reform and progress at every turn.

Governors of Virginia are elected every four years and are prohibited from serving consecutive terms. This renders them weaker than governors in many other states. More importantly for Devereaux, it enhances the power of legislative leaders, such as the ones which soon would be kissing his tassel loafers.

That weekend, Jack and Geraldine planned to entertain dinner guests. Friday night, they had the pleasure of Mary Jane Devereaux's company, and Sunday brunch planned to host Jack's mother Corrine. The weekend afforded a fine opportunity for Jeri to bond with two very important soon-to-be in-laws. For Jack it was the perfect family weekend: no Thomas, and no Courtney. Mary Jane arrived Friday evening straight after work from Charlottesville. Sweaters, designer jeans, and an avalanche of shoes were her signature wardrobe. With her heals she was almost as tall as Jeri, the two women walking evenly into an easy embrace at the front door. Jack gave his sister the usual tight bear hug, signifying their complete affection toward one another.

Like his two beloved dinner companions, the Judge was in a contented mood. Family and loved ones provide a unique and necessary shield against an indifferent and often meaningless world. Though Jack had recently taken hold of the world around him and kicked it in the balls, he understood this truth better than most. Even the strongest and most willful of men need a wife, whose loving arms and compassion he may escape into at any moment. Devereaux had that in Geraldine. He had grown up with an adopted older sister who never hesitated to take him in her arms and tell him he was the most important person in the world to her. His mother smothered and spoiled him rotten. And she protected him from his father's judgement and wrath.

Having had no brothers, his significant relationships had always been with women. But in school and college, Jack found it easy to make friends. He excelled at sports, impressed his fellows with his seemingly innate ability to charm the ladies, and possessed a self-confidence so overpowering that he was actually approachable; much more so than many of the other stiff privileged kids.

As the climax of the evening approached, Devereaux drank coffee with his fiancée and sister. While the women talked more, he took a cruise down memory lane trying to piece the puzzle of his life together. Despite the hyper success he had enjoyed as a boy, a student, and a man about town, there was that several years of appearing as a loose ship in the harbor with no direction.

As previously mentioned, Devereaux was a lackluster performer in the business and legal world when he first started out. But how could this happen to a young man who had every advantage and knew what he wanted? Jack didn't fully understand it yet, but his privileges always came with imperious expectations from his father, Thomas. And herein lies a core truth about Judge Devereaux. He would have his successes, but in his way. No one, especially his father, would shoulder him with duties and expectations he didn't want. That would not be success at all; that would be a prison.

So, consciously and subconsciously, Devereaux used his law practice to bide his time for the right opportunities and to make himself the most envied socialite in the county. "What are you thinking about, dear brother?" asked an inquisitive Mary Jane.

"I think you already know the answer to that question," said Jack as he winked at her. Jeri got up to clear the dining room table as her fiancé and soon-to-be sister gazed into each other's eyes, oblivious to the special and secretive love that Jack and Mary Jane still shared. Jeri knew that Mary Jane was adopted. What she did not know was that before his twelfth birthday, Jack's love for his adopted sister had turned obsessive. No girl or woman, including his ex-wife, could measure up to Mary Jane. No boyfriend of hers could escape his ire and hostility. It proved unnecessary, for Mary Jane would shower her favorite boy with unbridled affection every time she came home from a date.

It was almost as if she felt guilty being romantic with anyone. They never engaged in any inappropriate behavior. She was too good, and he thought her much too pure to ever sully the woman he worshipped with any carnal advances. You might say theirs was a medieval courtly love, forbidden and never fully acted upon. This might help to explain why Devereaux could never get close to another woman. He charmed, he lured, and he had his way with an untold amount of local young ladies, and from college. His romantic conquests were vast and superficial. When he married the young woman his father had arranged for him, Jack elevated his rakish activities to an astonishing level—for his wife was no Mary Jane. She was cold and unaffectionate, like his father.

When he met and hired Geraldine to be his legal secretary, it was superficial on his part. But happily for the two of them, they grew to love each other in a very short time. Jeri was not Mary Jane either, but she was uniquely wonderful, authentic, and true. She fell first, but Devereaux was lovestruck not too long afterwords. And Mary Jane could not be happier for her Jack and for a woman she had come to adore. "Let me help you, sweetheart," she said to Jeri. "Let His Honor enjoy his glass of port."

"Don't encourage him; he drinks too much as it is," Jeri joked.

Jack went outside and drank on the front porch. He had given Frank the weekend off and relished the privacy and slow pace of the evening. As he stepped inside to grab the port bottle, he heard the revving up sound of a car engine. He just smiled as he sat back down in the porch swing. It wasn't that long ago that he was a teenager in love with his speed mobile. In Warrenton,

Virginia, being a wealthy place, there was no shortage of young men with expensive fast cars financed by their parents. As his surroundings began to slip out of focus, Jack noticed a gray Dodge Charger pull up in front of the house. It was a loud and fast car, most impressive to look at. The passenger window came down and a young girl leaned out.

"Hey, stud! Come for a ride with us," she said with the full pitch of a screaming cheerleader. Jack tipped his glass to the girl and gently motioned for her to leave. The car sped off, screeching its tires.

"I'm glad I'm still young, but not that young," said Devereaux to himself. *Where do they get all that energy?* he thought. He finished all the port wine in the bottle, and as he rose to go into the house the gray car came back and again stopped in front of the house. This time, it revved and revved, but nobody appeared. The windows were rolled up and tinted. Jack suddenly became angry at having his peace disturbed.

He walked down the small flight of steps onto the walkway and down to the curb. "Do you know who I am?" the judge barked. "I own this street. Now get the fuck out of here before I have you pinched." As Devereaux banged on the hood of the car, the driver quickly emerged and shot him twice with an automatic pistol, then frantically sped off.

The shots knocked the judge down, but by some miraculous concoction of strength, belligerence, and good luck, he got back up off the ground and staggered all the way to the front porch. Then he collapsed.

CHAPTER 8

The five-mile ambulance ride to the hospital was emotional torment like none other for both of the judge's favorite ladies. "Oh, my boy. My sweet boy. My sweet, sweet angel," sobbed Mary Jane as the paramedic ordered her to sit down so he could attend to Jack.

Jeri was more subdued, not saying a word, but her tears streamed down her face like a waterfall. The ambulance arrived with a special contingent of Sheriff's Deputies accompanying the staff of doctors and nurses. Jack was semiconscious and breathing heavily, and the medical personnel rushed him into surgery prep with lightning speed. As Jeri and Mary Jane saw him disappear into the surgical quarters, they sat down in the waiting room and collapsed into each other's arms. They cried and hugged each other for so long that neither of them noticed Jeri's cell phone going off. It was McSherry trying to gently warn Jeri that he needed to ask her and Mary Jane some questions, even in their grievous conditions.

Frank didn't bother to play phone tag; he rushed to the hospital straight from the crime scene, which he had secured with all dispatch. Not wanting to interrupt the ladies comforting one another, he quietly pulled up a chair to offer his affections and sorrow. "Did any of you see anything when you noticed the judge on the porch? Anything at all?"

Jeri just admitted to being in the kitchen cleaning up and heard Mary

Jane scream. That's when the two went out to tend to Jack and call 911. Jeri had had the presence of mind to call Frank directly. The smell of the powerful sanitizer in the hospital was palpable enough for Frank to prop open a side door to the left of the waiting room. Observing how upset the women were, he decided to sit with them quietly for a bit. The facility they were in was brand new, with comfortable chairs and big-screen televisions. But nothing there could possibly distract Mary Jane and Jeri from the fact that they were in a hospital waiting for critical news concerning their beloved.

Just then, an elderly woman walked into the lobby. Seeing only the three in the waiting room, she approached. Jeri instantly recognized her as her neighbor from across the street. "Mrs. Farnham? What are you doing here?" asked a distraught Jeri.

"I'm so sorry, Geraldine. I just heard. This is absolutely awful. Such a young man! Is this gentleman a police officer?"

"Yes, Mrs. Farnham, I'm Sergeant McSherry," said Frank as he showed the woman his badge. "Do you have anything to tell me, ma'am?"

Mrs. Farnham sat down and relayed her recollections of the evening just prior to the shooting. "Whoever did this must have been very careful to see that none of us neighbors were on our porches or looking outside from our living rooms. Indeed, I didn't notice anything just prior to the shots. Neither did anyone else on the street with whom I talked just before coming over here. But something funny happened just before I sat down to dinner earlier in the evening. It was about 5:30 p.m. I ate in my living room so I could watch television and was facing toward the window with a view of the street. I can't tell you why I noticed it, but a dark gray sports car drove slowly up and down the street several times. I wasn't looking for anything in particular, you see. But as I ate my supper, I remembered that I had seen that same car parked up the street yesterday and the day before. I had never seen it before then. I don't think it belonged in the neighborhood."

"Can you give me more of a detailed description of the car, Mrs. Farnham?" asked Frank.

"Well, I got curious and put on my glasses the day before and noticed it was definitely gray with dark windows, and I could see *Dodge* written on the back."

McSherry patted the old woman on her hands, thanked her, and excused himself abruptly to make a call. "It's McSherry. Put out an all-points on a gray Dodge Charger or Dodge Challenger with tinted windows. No telling where they are—just ride up and down the main roads and check every neighborhood and shopping center. Everywhere, got it?" Frank sat back down with Mary Jane and Jeri.

Shortly thereafter, a deputy came up to Frank and the ladies and said, "The doctors say he's going to pull through. The bullets missed his heart completely but one hit his right lung. He might be laid up for a long time." Frank grabbed Jeri's hand, and Mary Jane hugged on Jeri tightly. The two women cried even harder but with some relief from the awfulness of the thing.

"May I go home now, Sergeant?" asked Mrs. Farnham. "My taxi is waiting outside."

"Ma'am, I will have this nice deputy drive you home and make sure your house is secure. Thank you for coming tonight, you've been very helpful."

"Geraldine, I'm thrilled that Judge Devereaux will be okay. You take it easy now," said a very concerned Mrs. Farnham.

"Thank you so very much," said Jeri as she kissed her neighbor goodnight. McSherry waited for two more officers to arrive at the hospital, giving them orders to stay with Jeri and Mary Jane. There were already two officers outside the operating room standing guard. Once all was secure at the hospital, Frank disappeared into the night to do what he did best.

Jeri slowly regained her composure and realized that nobody had notified Jack and Mary Jane's parents. Mortified, Jeri called Corrine and told her what happened. It was a great relief to be able to tell Mrs. Devereaux that her son would pull through. But what a close call!

"Should you call Courtney, Mary Jane?" Jeri asked.

"Like she'd actually care."

"Mary Jane," said Jeri softly. "Something horrible has happened in our family. Now is not the time..."

"I know, honey, I know."

Mary Jane rose and called her sister. Due to the lateness of the hour, both ladies recommended that the rest of the family wait until morning to come to the hospital. Surprisingly, everyone complied. When she got off the phone with Jeri, Corrine Devereaux was paralyzed with fear and grief. Naturally, she wanted Thomas to take her to the hospital immediately. Thomas agreed with Jeri, and the judge's parents sat tight for the night. Thomas comforted his wife and gave her a sedative. He left her in the bedroom and went downstairs to his study, poured himself a scotch, and sat down in his recliner. He thought of his son for the rest of the night. He pictured his boy in his judicial robes. He pictured a younger Jack riding horses and playing golf. Then he pictured his son as a little boy, then the baby that he and Corrine brought home to Bourbon Hill those many years ago. As Thomas Devereaux drank more, he thought more. And he wept painfully.

For reasons unknown, Mary Jane was unable to reach her younger sister. The Mansfields would have to be content with a voice message. The older Devereaux sister was now as alert as anyone could be in such circumstances. She noticed that despite dodging the worst of possibilities, Jeri was coming apart at the seams. So, she took charge of things.

"Jeri, come walk with me a few minutes. You have been in that chair half the night."

Jeri complied immediately as the two walked around the hospital hall by hall, room by room. Two sheriff's deputies were always behind them at a comfortable distance. "Sweetheart, I don't want this to sound like me giving orders, but I must insist that you come live at Bourbon Hill for a while," Mary Jane said. Before Jeri could speak Mary Jane spelled it all out: "Mother will have a room ready for Jack as soon as he is discharged from the hospital. Even if he has subsequent rehab, I know her. She will prepare the house for live-in nurses, if that's required. If you think about it, Jeri, it makes sense. Your home is a crime scene until they catch whoever did this to Jack. And we would all fear for your safety if you returned there. No, I'm quite determined my dear. We will go and pack you up and go to Mom and Dad's. I will stay with you. I can commute to my office from Bourbon Hill; it's no problem. Say you'll do this, Jeri. Please say yes!"

"How can I say no, Mary Jane? Thank you!" The two women tightened their hold on one another, then they walked some more.

Just before dawn that morning, the state police radio heated up. "Patch me through to McSherry, now," said an impassioned state trooper, Kyle Richardson. Richardson was only three years on the job, and he patrolled the area from Warrenton to Charlottesville. Having spotted a car which was a dead ringer for the crime vehicle, he wanted to talk to the man who recruited and commanded him before he talked to anyone else.

"Richardson, McSherry here. What have you got?"

"I'm down in Albemarle, just outside Charlottesville. Hanover Street, a side road off Route 29, small white farmhouse with two cars around back. One of them is a gray Dodge Charger with tinted windows."

"Richardson, we might be the luckiest cops in the country if this is the right car. I'm less than one hour away. Get out of sight and watch that house. Do not move unless they move. If they move, tail them discreetly."

"Roger that," said Richardson.

The trooper passed a very boring and uneventful 45 minutes when McSherry arrived on the scene. "I'll sneak around the back of the house. Wait five minutes and then pull up their driveway, so they can see your squad car and knock on the front door. Then immediately stand to the right of the door in case anybody gets the bright idea to shoot."

"Yes, sir."

It all went down just as Frank thought it might. Trooper Richardson knocked, then nothing. Within two minutes, a young man and even younger woman bolted the farmhouse from the rear and headed toward the Charger. McSherry stood up from behind the car with his pistol drawn. "Police, freeze and hands up!"

The woman screamed hysterically and threw herself to the ground. Her companion panicked as Richardson entered the backyard holding a shotgun. What was going on in the mind of the possible assailant was anyone's guess. Instead of surrendering right then and there, he stupidly ran away from McSherry, holding a pistol, and ran smack into Trooper Richardson who blasted him with his shotgun at close range, blowing every vital organ out of his chest cavity. Both men were instantly disturbed by this, for they obviously wanted to take the man alive for questioning.

By now, the woman got up, and in an avalanche of hysterics, rushed toward Richardson. Seeing that she was unarmed, McSherry rushed her before Richardson might have to shoot her. He grabbed her, and she swung at him screaming at the top of her lungs. Then McSherry punched her dead in the face. The concussion calmed her down considerably, and she began to cry as McSherry cuffed her and put her in Richardson's squad car. "This bitch knows something, Richardson," said an angry McSherry. "Take her to the Sheriff's office in Warrenton. I'll meet you there."

"Right-o, Chief."

Frank was not the slightest bit relieved. His detective mind told him that even if these unsavory characters were involved in Judge Devereaux's shooting, someone else had to have been behind it. He had one suspect to interrogate; that's all. And he wanted to make the most of it. So, he called the Sheriff of Fauquier County and briefed him in full. The Sheriff assured

Frank that he would have full resources and cooperation. Whoever did this to Judge Devereaux would be elevated to Public Enemy #1.

Fauquier County Deputy Amanda Beltran was a very pretty young woman with a very disarming personality. She would be the good cop to McSherry's bad cop. When everyone arrived at the station, Deputy Beltran took the female suspect into a holding room, gave her some hot coffee, and then allowed the girl to use the restroom. "Take as long as you need, sweetie," said the Deputy. When the girl returned, she told Deputy Beltran her name.

She was Natalie Rodriguez from Charlottesville, Virginia. She was 19 years old and lived with her mother. And she admittedly spent most of her time with her boyfriend, Randy Westover, now deceased. "Now I want you to relax and ready yourself to answer some questions, Natalie, okay? Don't be afraid. A judge has been shot, and everyone here needs to get to the bottom of this. Nobody is accusing you of anything, alright?" Beltran was most convincing, and the young and hopelessly ignorant suspect was calm and ready to be served up to McSherry.

"Miss Rodriguez, do you have any idea how much trouble you're in?" Frank barked. Natalie turned to Deputy Beltran in disbelief. Beltran just shrugged. Good cop would remain in the interrogation room, but bad cop would run the show. "I ran the history on your boyfriend. Drug dealing, aggravated assault, assault with a deadly weapon. What were you doing with this loser?"

Natalie, thinking of her dead boyfriend, began crying again. "He was a sweet man! He loved me, and you bastards shot him. He had nothing to do with your judge. Why can't I just go home?" Natalie got control of her tears and then got belligerent with Frank. That was a mistake.

"Look, you fucking criminal cockroach. I know your boyfriend and his car were at Judge Devereaux's house. Now, you start cooperating with me or we'll break some of your bones."

Shocked to the core, Natalie turned again to Deputy Beltran, who she thought was her friend. "Don't look at me, sweetie. This man is in charge." Then Beltran suddenly became the bad cop. "Look, bitch," she said as she grabbed Natalie by the hair. "You either tell us something or we throw you in a hole. And trust me, nobody around here will lift a finger to help you. For starters, you can rat out your dead boyfriend. What were he and his car doing in Warrenton last night?"

Natalie Rodriguez began to accept that she had no friends, her boyfriend was gone forever, and the scariest police officers in the world were ready to hang an attempted murder rap around her neck. Sobbing, she was at least able to utter the words, "Rich white guy, big money, one hit job, and then we could live in the Bahamas."

"How did Randy know this rich white guy?"

"I don't know," pleaded Natalie.

"Miss Rodriguez, you have one opportunity to save your own skin," said McSherry. "You're going to help us find this rich white guy. Understood?"

"What if I can't?" Natalie snapped.

"Then you're going to jail for attempted murder," said McSherry.

"Okay, I'll do whatever you want," Natalie cried. "Just don't yell at me anymore." She started crying again, and the two officers left her in the room.

"Nice interrogation, Officer Beltran! You should come work for me," winked McSherry.

It was an exceptionally good interrogation, particularly given the limited suspects and evidence then available. But a mountain of labor was still to be done. Questions remained: Who shot Judge Devereaux? Probably Randy Westover. Who paid Westover to do it? Anyone's guess!

CHAPTER 9

Two Months Later

J ack Devereaux didn't know it yet, but he was about to be entitled the Baron of Bourbon Hill. As the hot August afternoon descended over the Virginia Piedmont like an airborne sauna, the young judge put the finishing touches on his recovery. He was off the pain killers, so he could drink with impunity (which he did, day and night). His lung had healed so quickly that his doctors and nurses thought divine intervention was at play. He could breathe deeply without much discomfort and was told he could begin exercise in a couple of weeks.

As for work, he would return the following Monday, so restless was he. When Jack got up to fix another drink, his wife intervened. "If you insist on drinking scotch in the middle of the day, at least let me get it for you, darling."

"If you insist," grinned the judge. He probably planned it that way, anyhow. Jeri, Mary Jane, and his mother had been pampering the young man since he came home to Bourbon Hill from the hospital. As the couple spent the afternoon talking about their wedding plans, Thomas Devereaux was downstairs in his study, where he had been laboring since breakfast. Jeri came up with a fresh scotch, and as she handed it to Jack his father came in right behind her.

"Geraldine, I need a word with my son. Please go and sit with Corrine in the sunroom for a few minutes." Jeri obliged, and a puzzled Jack sipped his spirits.

"Before I tell you what I've been doing the past few days, I want your word as a gentleman and as a Devereaux that you will lay off your sister."

"I don't suppose you mean Mary Jane," chuckled Jack.

"You know I mean Courtney, you wise ass," Thomas snapped. "Now, I don't know, and I have stopped caring entirely about the reason for your hatred of each other. But it stops now. Do not interfere with her marriage again, even though you delude yourself that you've been defending her husband. Leave them both alone," barked Thomas as he snatched the scotch glass from his son and chugged it himself. "I know it was you who set up that drunk driving incident."

"How could you know that, Pop?"

"Where do you think you get your smarts from, son?"

"From Mom?"

"Knock it off, boy, or I might just change my mind about what I have done for you." Intrigued, Jack sat back in his chair and listened respectfully to his father. "Courtney will do whatever I tell her to do. I have coddled her and failed to drop the axe on her many times over the years. That's my fault, but your hostility toward her is your problem. And you're going to fix it today."

"What do you want, Pop?"

"I want your ironclad word that you no longer bear your sister any ill will. And that you promise never to do her any harm or dishonor. Promise it now, son." The father's face grew stern, and his eyes burned right through Jack's face. It was abundantly clear the old man meant business.

"All right, Pop. If she doesn't do or say anything dishonorable to myself, Jeri, or Mary Jane, then I will keep the peace on my end."

As Thomas heard these words of Jack's, he tossed himself into the other easy chair and sighed with a relief that stemmed from years of agony and disgust. Not just of his daughter's behavior and his failure to restrain it, but from the clear-cut malice that existed between his children. He also knew that his relationship with his son had suffered for many reasons, one of which was that Jack and his father were virtual clones of one another in their capacity for detestation. If either father or son hated you, you stayed hated for a long time. Thomas regained his business-like countenance and handed Jack a paper that most men on earth would kill for. It gave Jack sole and complete title to the family estate, Bourbon Hill. Lands, mansion house, and outbuildings. Sixteen-hundred and seventy-two acres worth at least $100 million.

No sooner had Jack read the papers than a lightning storm blew into the county. A dark, dark cloud began to hover over the estate producing ferocious wind and rain. The thunder silenced the two men for nearly an hour, and when the storm passed, the electricity was out, and trees were down. Thus, the spectacular entitlement bestowed upon Judge Jack Devereaux appeared to have the endorsement of the most ominous storm of the season. The moment was positively gothic!

"Where are you going, Pop?"

"Downstairs to get us both another whiskey," said the old man calmly. In the few minutes it took for Thomas Devereaux to retrieve the next round, the judge worked out a very definitive change of mind toward his father. He had always respected Thomas's competence, good manners, and gentility. Now he had just witnessed the raw exercise of power from a rich and powerful man. Thomas had not called a family meeting. He had not sought outside counsel. He simply got agreement from his wife and then singlehandedly bequeathed a grand Virginia estate to his only son.

Thomas and Corrine would have a life estate on the property and would take additional measures to avoid the huge inheritance taxes the children would be obliged to pay. Jack smiled, much contented with his improved circumstances but also of the ease with which his father operated. He was grateful. He was even relieved to be able to junk his nefarious plans he had in store for Courtney, for he no longer had any need to bring ruin upon her. But it was the power that made his day. Jack always had plenty of money, or access to it. But becoming Lord of the Manor increased his power immediately, and exponentially. And power was something which interested Jack Devereaux.

As Thomas returned to the bedroom with the whiskeys, his son was in deep thought. Half his brain questioned why he hadn't listened to his father more, and at a younger age. This was a direct corollary of his now elevated opinion of Thomas. The other half of his brain dismissed the first by a simple understanding that Jack could not labor at the direction of other people. He could never have done as Thomas directed; not just because it would have interfered with his hedonism, but because it would have made him feel subjugated. In the bluntest of terms, Jack was opposed to the very idea of service. Apart from doing favors for people he liked or loved, serving was anathema to him. This included his position as circuit judge. Not for one minute did Devereaux consider himself a public servant. It was the power of the job only which appealed to him.

So it was that Jack Devereaux passed the first test of power gamesmanship in his mind when he insisted on working for and serving himself. The man that is his own boss is by definition a powerful man. Having money is indifferent to this principle apart from the fact of enabling the requisite independence. Jack drank his whiskey, and every devious bone in his body danced a jig. Two months ago, he was left for dead, and now he had it all. "What about Mary Jane and Courtney? Aren't they going to feel slighted that I got mine in advance?" inquired the judge. He saw his father's hesitation and instantly foreshadowed the response.

"They have trust funds, son. Very, very large ones. I'm going to add significantly to the annual amount for them both," Thomas said.

"I figured as much," Jack said. "You never gave me one because you wanted me out of the will. You must have known that for a long time."

"As far as I am concerned, this is now ancient history. You've gotten your act together, boy—judgeship and a pretty incredible bride-to-be. You deserve this!"

The last comment took Jack off guard, for he had never heard his father say that he deserved anything, saving a whipping or two. "I've been over the books with Mom several times over the years, Pop. She asked me to help her understand the family assets. Where did you get the cash for trust funds?"

"From several offshore accounts that you need know nothing about. They don't concern you."

Jack glanced at his father and tipped his scotch glass. He would never ask Thomas about his financial intricacies again. But his newfound respect for Thomas was elevated even more. It appears that his stern, thrifty, and ethically fussy father had no problem dodging taxes and washing his money in foreign places.

"Well, son, your mother and I are driving to Charlottesville now that the storm is over. Antiquing! You have a good rest."

As Thomas left the room, Jack smiled again. He asked himself a question. "If Pop breaks these kinds of laws with considerable ease, then hasn't he been a hypocrite demanding ethical purity from me all these years? Maybe so, maybe so. Does it bother me? Surprisingly no!" The internal dialog occupied Jack for several hours that turbulent afternoon. He concluded that he had not been a rascal and rule-breaker just to get back at his dad. How did he know that? Because he was now more determined than ever to wield power, and to maliciously violate every rule in the book doing it.

The shooting had not left Jack with any special revelations, spiritual awakenings, or renewed commitments to appreciate life in the mundane. No, he was more or less the same person he was when he was shot, except for this greatly enhanced will to power. Thomas Devereaux would never fully grasp the significance of his timing. He was ready to give, and Jack was even more ready to receive. Jack did not expect any grandiose apologies or further gestures from Thomas. He knew the real reason for his father's actions that day.

It had little to do with his becoming a judge or marrying Geraldine. It was because Jack had been shot and could have died. Thomas had acted out of sadness and guilt. And Jack was fine with that.

Courtney visited Bourbon Hill the next day. She and Jack buried the proverbial hatchet, perhaps adding some years to the lives of their parents. She seemed unconcerned when told of Jack's early inheritance. Her husband was rich, and she was forever in her father's good graces, and the will. However, a man like Judge Devereaux thrives on conflict. His chief personal vengeance was on hold, for there had been no further breaks in the case of who had paid a man to shoot him.

His little sister had just removed a major source of conflict from him. Though it was a fair trade for what he received, his emotions would not be at rest until he replaced that hatred and directed it toward another person or persons. He had the coming weekend to finish his recovery; then it would be back to the office and the bench, where he might fill the villainous void with his venal scheming and high-handed dispensing of justice. This he would no doubt enjoy. But it would be news from Detective Frank McSherry that would set Jack firmly on the dark path. It would be welcome news, for it was the dark path which he wished to travel for a while.

CHAPTER 10

Judge Devereaux entered his chambers Monday morning and received warm greetings from his staff. In his office, he noticed a case of bourbon in front of his private desk. Glancing at the note his suspicions were confirmed. It was a present from the Chief Judge. As Detective McSherry walked in, he eyed the expensive liquor. "We'll have to elevate the Chief to the status of a friend. This is some mighty fine bourbon, Judge."

"Indeed it is, Frank. Make sure there are no new security cameras around here, will you?" As Devereaux sat down to peruse the motions document and other court papers, McSherry came back in.

"Found two fresh hidden cameras, Judge," Frank said.

Devereaux thought a moment. "Don't say anything to the Chief Judge— just quietly disable them. Let's see how fast they come back and fix them. Also, sweep this office and the lobby for any other devices."

"Will do," McSherry said.

Courtroom security had been greatly enhanced in recent years. The old country courthouse was beginning to echo the federal courts in its sophistication and safety apparatus. It was probably just a simple case of the Chief of the Circuit wanting his court rooms to mimic the models of secure fortresses that comprised the urban areas of the country. But for

Jack Devereaux, closed circuit television was an innovation with which he was unprepared to welcome, for two reasons. The first being the obvious need for secrecy. And secondly, true men of power do not get monitored daily by other people. It is a matter of principle.

Frank McSherry returned to the office with a briefcase. He closed the door and pulled out an electronic stick device. Within minutes, he cleared the judge's office for any bugs then the lobby. After disconnecting the closed-circuit TV wires, he and Devereaux began the paramount conversation of the day. The call girls, according to Frank, had done some serious damage. None other than the Speaker of the Virginia House of Delegates was on videotape with two of the girls in a Richmond hotel just a block from the State Capital.

"The man you will see in the tapes, Judge, is a man over 60 years old. He's married with kids and grandkids. And his political persona is one of extreme social conservatism; a real family values man."

"My curiosity gets the better of me sometimes, Frank. What's on the tape?"

"Only this kindly old grandpa having kinky sex with two young women under 30."

"Oh, Frank. As a welcome-back present, this beats the bourbon by a mile," grinned the Judge. "We just bagged the elephant on the first go around. What about the Senate leaders, the State Police, and Bureau of Prisons Chief?"

"Nothing yet, Judge. The Speaker is the only one to take the bait so far," Frank said.

"How soon can you get the tapes operational?"

"By tonight, hard drive and back-up."

The judge thought for a few seconds and then picked up his phone. "Mama, how well do you and Pop know the Virginia House Speaker?"

"Quite well, darling. His wife is in the Daughters of the American

Revolution with me."

"Ha-ha, when it rains, it pours," Devereaux whispered to Frank as he placed his hand on the phone's receiver. "Will you do me a great favor and invite them to Bourbon Hill for a nice dinner—say the week after next? And drop a hint of a campaign contribution. Jeri and I will be there, but don't tell anyone. We'll surprise them!"

"Of course, dear, if you think it might help you," said a most cooperative Corrine.

"Thank you, Mama. It should be an enlightening evening. Uh-huh, bye."

McSherry sat there in awe of his boss again. He just could not imagine a man so young playing games of this magnitude with such prowess and ease.

"It's early in the day, Frank, but why don't we sample some of the Chief Judge's bourbon." Frank smiled as he opened a bottle and poured.

"You know, Frank, I highly recommend getting shot. No one has refused a favor request from me since this thing happened." The two men laughed heartily and sipped some damn fine whiskey at 11:00 in the morning.

"What are we going to do about the House Speaker?" Frank asked.

"I haven't worked out the details yet, but he's going to be a gift that continues to give." The two laughed even harder and drank more.

Two uneventful weeks on the bench passed without Judge Devereaux missing a beat. He accepted some motions, denied others, and put six men in prison. The main point is that he was back in the saddle, as they say. Two weeks on the job for the youngest and most charismatic judge in the circuit was more than sufficient to erase the previous two months of absence. Fauquier County was back to normal, save for the fact that whoever hired the late Randy Westover to shoot the judge was still at large. Would they try again? Would they ever be caught? Devereaux was unconcerned with this detail. The full weight of state and local law enforcement prioritized catching this conspirator. Besides, Jack and Jeri were living at a very secure and guarded estate, and he had the best security man in the business shadowing him daily. The Sheriff's Office and Warrenton Town Police proved beyond doubt, based on the forensic evidence, that Westover was the shooter and that his girlfriend was with him. She cooperated as fully as a drugged-up school dropout was able to. Natalie Rodriguez had ridden with her boyfriend to Warrenton that night but had no idea why. When Westover shot the judge, she thought it was because of a simple altercation. She was so high on heroin when she was arrested that she could provide only fragments of a conversation Westover had had on his phone.

She couldn't remember much before the interview at the police station, which had frightened her. Thus, the only information the authorities got out of her was that her boyfriend said a rich white guy had given him a job to do. Charged as an accessory to attempted murder, Natalie was in jail at the county lock-up awaiting trial. On a sleepy Friday afternoon, she was escorted to an obscure and unused interrogation room with no cameras. Upon entering, she was terrifyingly startled to be face to face again with Detective Sergeant Frank McSherry. Shaking like a leaf, she begged the deputy to return her to her cell. The deputy closed the door and left.

"Hello, Natalie. Don't be afraid. I'm not going to harm you. I'm here to let you know that you have friends."

"Like who?" inquired the young girl.

"Me, for starters," retorted McSherry. "I have a little present for you," he said as he produced a small bag of heroin and put it in her hand.

"Are you trying to get me in trouble? They search us every day for this stuff," said an increasingly disturbed Natalie.

"Not anymore, at least not you, Miss Rodriguez. I, or someone using my name, will be by to see you twice a week. Make this stuff last, okay?"

"Why are you doing this?" Natalie asked.

"I told you: you have friends." McSherry quickly exited the room.

Natalie devoured all of the heroin, wondering if she could trust that she wouldn't be searched. She was not. She was escorted back to her cell without incident. And waited very impatiently for her next fix.

That late Saturday afternoon sported a perfect weather day at Bourbon Hill. Sunny, low humidity, 72 degrees and dropping by the hour. The Speaker of the Virginia House and his wife, Helen, turned into the driveway and passed through the now famous black iron gate. Though early autumn, the magnificent trees, bushes, and shrubs outlining the estate's front yard were still leafed out and bright green, due to the light rainfall from the summer months. The large pond to the right of the driveway provided a rare sighting for the visitors. As they parked the car and headed for the front door, two bald eagles circled the left edge of the pond, making no noise but commanding the air and the bright blue sky with a majestic sketch that no camera could easily capture. The eagles set their wings and began the evening watering and bedding down process.

Before the couple could recover from the sight, a Cooper's Hawk, larger than normal, screeched and landed on the roof above the front door. As it took its perch, the hawk held its head and beak high and arrogantly, spying the grounds of Bourbon Hill with a predator's eye. Its white chest projected center mass atop the mansion house. As the guests were warmly greeted by the senior Devereauxs, the politician took another glance at the hawk before disappearing into the massive foyer of the house. His wife had entertainment on her mind, but the politician's thoughts were still of the birds of the air. While the eagles were quite a sight but soon forgotten, the Cooper's Hawk was an image which would remain plastered on his psyche all night.

"Well, Helen...It is a pleasure to be with you at a place outside those long, long DAR meetings," expressed a happy and hospitable Corrine Devereaux. "And Bill, I don't think we've all been together like this for a decade. Welcome! Go on into the parlor where Thomas is. I want to show

Helen our new veranda."

"Mr. Speaker, I believe bourbon and branch is still your poison?" Thomas asked.

"Always, Thomas, always." The men sat down and drank their first cocktail, then the whole room grew quiet as Geraldine Pike descended the staircase in a short black dress. Her hair was teased to one side and held with a comb. Her hips bounced elegantly and succulently, back and forth, back and forth.

"Good afternoon, I'm Jeri," she said to the Speaker as she offered her hand. The Speaker, mouth agape, gently grabbed her hand.

"It is a distinct honor, Miss, or shall I say the soon-to-be Mrs. Devereaux?"

Jeri blushed as she always did when she thought of herself as Mrs. Devereaux. Thomas gave her a drink and the three enjoyed 20 minutes or so of idle chit chat. Just as the drinks began to flow and the environment grew carefree, the predator got loose and descended upon the party. And it wasn't the Cooper's Hawk.

"Mr. Speaker, good evening," said Judge Devereaux with a winning smile and flushed face, straightening the bow tie which accentuated his Italian handcrafted Tuxedo. "Pop, let me refresh your drink."

The Speaker had been quite relaxed the moment he arrived at Bourbon Hill but was not informed that the judge and his fiancée would be there. He had expected, as was customary, for Thomas Devereaux to quietly hand him an envelope with a considerable check while they were alone drinking. Then Geraldine entered the room, then Jack Devereaux.

I shouldn't be at a private family dinner with a judge I may have to reappoint, thought the Speaker to himself. *And when in the hell am I going to get my money?* A master politician in his own right, the legislative leader concealed his displeasure and engaged the young couple with charm and enthusiasm, regaling them with political stories from the good ole days.

Dinner was served promptly at 7 p.m. "Bill, I believe roast duck with an apricot glaze is your favorite," Corrine said as the caterers brought out the main course.

"Oh, indeed it is, Corrine. I believe it was George Washington's favorite dish as well. You can still get it at the Mount Vernon Inn Restaurant these days. Though I can't imagine they do it as well you, my dear."

Helen, the Speaker's wife, echoed the sentiment, and everyone enjoyed a fine and proper Virginia evening. Thomas was the first to break his own rule of not discussing politics at the dinner table. "Bill, I understand the other party is making inroads in Richmond and the surrounding counties. That can't be good for you and the boys."

"It's all these northerners moving down here and bringing their damn fool ideas with them, Thomas. We're having a hard time competing for their votes."

Jack sipped his wine as he glared at the Speaker. "Why don't you just lean on our friends on the Boards of Supervisors and Zoning Commissions, tell them to stop approving large housing projects? That alone would slow down the migrants from up north. Unless you're afraid of the builders and real estate folks," suggested a smug Judge Devereaux.

"Now, Jack, be careful. You may have to rule on a legal matter concerning these very issues. We shouldn't be discussing them." The Speaker asked for more wine, his hands shaking; he was palpably disturbed by Jack's blatant political overtones. Partly because judges are supposed to attempt to be non-partisan, but mostly because he saw Thomas smiling proudly at everything his boy was saying. It was at that very moment the Speaker knew he had stepped into a well-laid trap. He was confident that he would not leave Bourbon Hill that night without giving the Devereauxs something momentous in return for the financial contribution he had yet to receive.

Fortunately for the continued gentility of the evening, Geraldine placed her hand gently on the Speaker's knee. "I understand your mother's family is from Savannah. My mother lives there, Bill. Ah, my, can I call you Bill?" inquired Jeri slyly.

"Oh, yes to both questions, pretty lady!"

The Speaker made his hosts endure a long stemwinder of southern history as experienced by his family. But the mood in the room was greatly enhanced by Jeri's intervention, and dinner dragged on well past 9 p.m. Just as all at the table were enjoying dessert and expensive port, a knock at the door startled the party. "Who got past our gate, Thomas?" asked a concerned Corrine.

"It's my security chief," said Jack. "I buzzed him in through my phone. Let me handle this. Excuse me a moment." The judge let Frank McSherry into the foyer, asking him to take a seat. "Mr. Speaker, will you join the Detective Sergeant and myself on the patio where we can have some privacy? I'm sorry, but there is some urgent state police business that needs our attention." Silence engulfed the dinner table as Jack led the Speaker out into the foyer, introducing him to McSherry, and the three men disappeared to the patio.

"I'll get right to it, Mr. Speaker," said McSherry as he tapped a large yellow envelope. "We've uncovered a prostitution ring in Richmond which appears to be targeting state officials."

The Speaker swallowed hard that very second, trying desperately not to look at the envelope in McSherry's hand. "Um, uh, do you mean members of the legislature?"

Frank paused, glanced briefly at Judge Devereaux, and then directed his attention to the Speaker. "I'm afraid so, in addition to executive officials as well. This investigation is ongoing, and we will need your cooperation; secretly of course."

Devereaux, at that point, took over the conversation as McSherry handed the Speaker the envelope. "Bill, you have friends. Friends in this house, friends right here on this patio. Do you understand?"

The Speaker's heart raced even faster than his nervous and anxious mind. He knew very well what was in that envelope, sure as day, but he attempted to regain his composure and looked at the photographs he pulled out.

"She does have an exceptional butt, doesn't she, Bill? I believe you and I share the same fetish," said Devereaux as he pointed to the large photo showing the Speaker taking one of the girls from behind. "Relax, Bill. Frank, get him another drink, please." McSherry walked into the parlor and poured himself and the Speaker a glass of bourbon. "As the Sergeant said, there is an ongoing investigation as to the reach and magnitude of this prostitution ring. It obviously includes the motive of corrupting public officials. Extortion comes to mind as well," said Devereaux, just twisting the proverbial knife. "Easy does it. Nobody's going to blow the whistle on you, Bill. These photographs never have to see the light of day. Hell, I'm not even going to ask you to do anything risky for me," said the Judge as Frank handed the Speaker a whiskey.

"What is it you want, Judge?" the Speaker asked as he sank into his chair, visibly defeated.

"Nothing more than for you to keep doing the tremendous job you're doing as speaker of our fair state house. And whenever Frank or I ask you for a favor, you do it! Do we have an understanding, Bill?"

"Yes, Judge, we do. I'm not feeling so well. I think it's time for the Missus and I to clear out now," said the Speaker. "I'm going to trust that you are a man of your word?"

"Yes, Bill, you can. Take our direction when required, and you can have a long career and a happy retirement. Oh, and don't forget your Devereaux family campaign contribution," exclaimed Jack as he handed the Speaker another envelope. Devereaux walked the Speaker around the side of the house to the other parlor where everyone was sitting. "I'm sorry we had to take Bill away from you, Helen. But our business is concluded," Jack said.

The Speaker wiped the sweat off his brow with a handkerchief, motioned to his wife, and thanked the Devereauxs for a memorable evening and bid them goodnight.

"I'll walk them to their car," said Thomas as he excused himself from Corrine and Geraldine.

"The Sergeant made a special trip here. I'll give him a nightcap and join you in a few minutes," Jack said. Corrine and Jeri look puzzled in light of the last hour's happenings. But they renounced concern in favor of enjoyment, sipping coffee and eating extra dessert.

When Devereaux and McSherry were on the patio out of earshot, Frank showered his boss with compliments. "I've never seen anyone operate as smoothly as you do, Judge," he said.

"Thank you, Frank. I will admit, that is how you handle a politician," Jack said. "And a friend at that, Frank!"

"I'd like to see more of how you handle an enemy, Judge."

"Fortunately for us both, you will be witness to such an event very shortly."

Devereaux grinned, Frank started to chuckle, and then the two conspirators laughed the laugh of victory and villainy.

CHAPTER II

Two naked and lustful figures lay next to each other, watching the sun come up from the master bedroom window at Bourbon Hill. Corrine and Thomas had given the room to Geraldine and Jack and moved into nearly equally luxurious lodgings at a downstairs bedroom on the far-right wing of the mansion. Jeri rested her head on the Judge's stomach, running her fingers up and down his chest. She paid close attention to the surgical scar still pronounced prominently below his right pectoral.

"What are you doing, pretty girl?" he said.

"Oh, just deciding whether that scar reduces you from perfection," sighed Jeri.

"And what is the verdict, Mrs. Devereaux?"

"Not one iota, dreamboat!"

Thanks in part to the total victory in his dealings with the House Speaker, Jeri became Mrs. Devereaux the following week. Jack whisked her away to the Green Spring Hotel in West Virginia on a whim and high. Perhaps the most opulent mountain resort east of the Mississippi, it was not a hard sell to get Thomas, Corrine, Mary Jane, Frank, and Mimi to stand up at a beautifully simple ceremony and three days of decadent pleasures at the hotel. In the spirit of cooperation, Jack invited Courtney and her husband, but they were vacationing in Europe and politely declined. Mimi had learned to be coy in dealing with Frank, a relationship she had come to value and was determined to honor. But it was all she could do to conceal her envy, fantasizing intensely about being Mrs. Devereaux herself. That aside, however, things were rosy in this tightknit group of family and friends.

Jack turned over and rested his head on Jeri's butt. Then he kissed her impressive cheeks and gently bit them. He was in his own world, working his way down the back of her legs, tickling and licking. Jeri moaned and sighed, but did not take her eyes off the simple but elegant platinum wedding ring which accented the diamond engagement ring on the same finger. It was a wonderfully mutual milestone they both passed, marrying their dream mates. "You are so open with your feelings, Mr. Devereaux," said Jeri. "You make me feel safe. But every now and then, I get the feeling you're hiding a thing or two. Not just from me, but from everyone."

"What brought this up, honey?" The judge was now fully awake, for his wife had gotten his attention in a non-sexual manner. "The only things I keep from you have to do with my job. There is a dirty underbelly about ruling and governing that I would rather keep you away from. Trust me, you'll be the happier for it. But if you insist, I will tell you anything you want to know." At once, Jack's muscles tensed up as he took a huge gamble that Jeri was becoming a need-to-know-everything wife. To his great relief, she said that she didn't need or even want to be privy to all the gory details of his work life.

"I do have one question that's piqued my curiosity. What was the real reason for having the House Speaker and his wife over here for dinner the week before last?"

"Well, I'm afraid all I have is a boring answer for you. It was for them to be wined and dined, receive a campaign donation, and to meet you and be charmed by us. That way, he is more committed to my reappointment than he was previously. Just plain old routine politics, darling. No hijinks."

Jeri was satisfied with his answer and went straight back to staring at her wedding ring, while Jack threw himself on top of her, tightly embracing his new wife. She hugged him back and the two remained in the warm embrace until Corrine sounded the alarm for breakfast and coffee. Fortunately, Jeri put on a long, thick robe to wear at the kitchen table, for just as the Devereauxs sat down to eat, Frank McSherry knocked at the side door.

"Come in, Mr. McSherry," directed a hospitable Corrine.

"I'm taking the day off, nothing in my courtroom today, Frank," Jack said.

"Whatever you say, Judge. If it's all the same, I'd like to shoot some crows over by the pond. I have my shotgun in the truck."

"Certainly, Frank, knock yourself out and stay for lunch. I want to meet with you for a few minutes before you leave this afternoon."

"Sure thing, Judge. Have a lovely morning. You too, Mrs. Devereaux, and Mrs. Devereaux!" The last salutation widened the smile on Geraldine's face.

The lovers returned to the scene of the crime and demonstrated the inexhaustible energy of two young people in love. They gave themselves over to one another with such purpose and clarity that they barely noticed the dozens of shotgun blasts coming from the pond. The judge and his bride soaked the bed sheets with their sweat, and after two more hours they lay on their backs, heads on their pillows, and took a good deal of time catching their breath. No additional workouts would be necessary that day. They fell asleep in each other's arms and did not wake until after 2 p.m.

As he woke, Jack remembered inviting Frank to stay for lunch. Nudging Jeri, he was met with strict orders to do lunch himself. His wife wanted more sleep. Jack ran downstairs and whipped up some coffee and sandwiches. He then gave McSherry a text message. Frank hit the side door to the kitchen just as the judge put the lunch plates on the table.

"I heard quite a bit of shooting out there. Kill anything?"

"Ten crows and about two dozen pigeons," Frank said. "I bagged them. They are in the truck. I think I will take them to the boys later today, Judge."

"Good idea. Don't hesitate to invite them over here for some hunting," Devereaux graciously offered.

"Now, down to business. I have something I want our friend, the Speaker, do for us. And I don't want to be seen in Richmond myself. Can you go down there on Thursday? He will be in his office that day; big bills being voted on. Don't alert him in advance. I want him off guard when you show up. Get there just before they break for lunch."

"Yes, sir," said Frank. "What am I supposed to relay to him?"

"Remember when I said that I have big plans for him?"

"Yes indeed," Frank replied.

"It begins this week, with the contents inside this letter." Jack handed Frank a sealed white envelope, and the men sported schoolboy grins on their faces. As McSherry left the mansion, he surmised that the House Speaker was about to earn his contribution from the Devereauxs. He almost felt sorry for the old politician.

The Kentucky Gauntlet was the name given to an annual sport by its chief participants. Every fall, the McSherry cousins, Sergeant Frank and brother Sheriff Brian, would invite an honored guest to the farm to "run the gauntlet." Based loosely on the Shawnee and Iroquois Indian gauntlets where a captive had to run through many men standing on both sides of a line and withstand crushing blows from feet, fists, and war clubs, the Kentucky version presented a splendid additional test of courage. The guest began at a spot 40 yards from the front of a barn. He would sprint through the five McSherry boys, who would punch, kick, or body check the man as hard as they wished. If the fortunate soul made it to the barn, the boys gave him five minutes to catch his breath. Then they gave him an extra-large Bowie knife, opened the barn door, and tossed him inside, where a wild boar had been turned loose. If the man killed the boar, he would participate in a special ritual with the McSherrys. The bloody knife was cleaned and used to slice the hands of all of the participants, who all pressed their hands against each other's, becoming blood brothers.

If the man ran out of the barn or failed to kill the dangerous animal within 30 minutes, he would have to wait until the following year to try again and hopefully become blood brother to the McSherry Clan. Though not in Kentucky that year, they still called for the gauntlet to be run. The cousins were game to have most anyone give it a try, but Frank McSherry's brother, the Sheriff of Buchanan County, put the screws to Frank to invite none other than Judge Devereaux.

At first, Frank was hesitant, given that it was only a couple of months since Devereaux had been shot. But the Sheriff wanted to see if a country gentleman like the judge was capable of any more hillbilly moxie than just plain old city folks. Frank was amazed to see Devereaux's eyes light up when he informed the judge of his invitation. "It will be at the farm with Brian and the boys," said Frank. "This Saturday, just before sundown, you run to the barn and take whatever we give you, including me. If you make it, we give you five minutes to catch your breath, then you go inside the barn with a knife and kill that boar."

Devereaux was speechless but smiling with anticipation. Here was a prime opportunity to elevate the men's respect and devotion toward him.

Frank continued, "Because you've been healing up from that gunshot, I'm going to tell you exactly how to succeed with this; that is, if you want to go ahead."

"Do I get to be a Kentucky Colonel and have a seat at the Derby?" asked Devereaux sarcastically.

"That would involve the Governor of Kentucky, so that's a big no." The men shared a laugh as McSherry gave the judge the key to running the gauntlet and killing the boar. "Cover your head with your arms and run lightly, don't sprint. Focus on getting to the barn and take the blows. Nobody will hit you in the chest where your wound was. Breathe deeply and stay calm when you reach the barn. When you're given the Bowie knife and go into the barn, you'll see an anxious and energetic boar. You'll be scared, but control your fear. When he's turned loose on you, run from side to side in the barn. Make him chase you for several minutes and wear him out."

"Won't I be worn out too, Frank?"

"Doesn't matter, Judge. This boar is not a man eater, but those tusks will chew your legs and feet something fierce. Anyway, drop to one knee if you need to catch your breath. Never lie down. When he charges you again, you'll see his head lowered. Reach out and plunge the knife in his head. Got it so far, Judge?"

"Yes, I think."

"Run away each time you stab him, then when he is on the ground and reasonably still, bury the knife in his torso, just above the front legs. Then, exit the barn with your knife. If you do this inside of 30 minutes, it counts, even if the boar takes a little longer to die."

Devereaux sat in his office chair in amazement. After a few deep breaths, he told Frank to set up the gauntlet run for Saturday. Was the Judge a bit crazy at that moment? Did being shot and any latent insecurity concerning his physical condition cause him to take such a chance? This was no mere sport, at least none that Jack ever encountered. Did he really need the admiration of the McSherrys that much? The answer was yes to all three! What really drove Judge Devereaux at that moment, though, was a sense of invincibility, of indestructibility. Surviving a point-blank shooting and becoming master of his family estate induced him to think in terms of a destiny for himself. What better way to prove his metal than to master this Kentucky Gauntlet?

The weather was dry and chilly that Saturday. The cousins readied the wild boar and had spent the day working out and doing a little bird hunting. Sheriff Brian McSherry was there with two of his deputies from Grundy, Virginia, about six hours southwest of the Piedmont in coal country on the border with Kentucky. Around 4:30 p.m., Frank arrived with their honored guest. The Sergeant shook hands with his brother, the deputies, and his cousins. Everyone drank a beer and exchanged pleasantries for a few minutes. Everyone except Jack, who got out of the car and stretched. He did not speak but simply nodded to everyone. Frank took the cue as he removed his jacket and gun holster.

"Let's get this thing started, boys," he said. The McSherrys lined up as Devereaux covered his head with his arms. He paused for a second, then began to jog through the men toward the barn. The first two blows from the cousins were heavy, knocking Devereaux back and forth, a third blow nearly knocked him down. Looking only at the barn door and not at the men impeding his progress to it, he felt himself breaking free, then he was kicked twice and absorbed an avalanche of punches from them all, including Frank, who had promised the judge that he would not hold back. No sooner had Jack been knocked down than he tapped into his deep-seated belligerence, got up, and ran forward. Sheriff McSherry was the last man on the line before the barn door. He threw two jabs and a roundhouse punch and knocked Devereaux to the ground.

The judge breathed deeply, coughed and grunted for a minute, then got back off the ground. He looked back at the Sheriff, then the cousins, then Frank. Visibly smiling, he walked the few yards over to the barn door and touched it.

"I never thought he would make it this far," said one of the cousins.

"You don't know this man like I do," said Frank. "He's not from our parts, but he damn sure is a survivor. The man got shot twice in the chest almost point blank. Now, here he is only three months later. Give me the knife." Frank walked over to Devereaux and gave him the Bowie knife. "Do you remember everything I told you, Judge?"

"Got it," said Jack as he breathed and spit.

"The boar is loose in the barn now. Ready?"

"Open the fucking door, Frank."

He may have been a judge, and a powerful, wealthy, and impressive one. But on that Saturday afternoon, the McSherry Clan just stared at him as he entered the barn. He knew he could never be considered one of them unless he killed that boar. As Frank shut the door, the last rays of sunlight were pouring in through the windows on either side. He heard the monster pig squeal seconds before. Now, Jack saw this heinous animal, all muscle and tusks, move toward him with increasing speed. He was more exhausted than terrified but managed to run wall to wall as Frank instructed. Each time he was out of breath and dropped to one knee to catch it. The boar slowed down as Jack got up. It charged again, only to be cut by Devereaux's knife. Being too tired to plunge, Jack had simply swung the huge knife and cut the boar in the ear.

Either fatigue, anxiety, or both overtook Jack, and he was certain he would have to call for help soon. He ran the four walls of the barn one last time and stopped to put his hands on his knees, panting heavily. The boar ran at him again and Jack had the presence of mind to notice his head was ducked. He gripped the Bowie knife tighter than ever, stepped toward the boar from a slight side angle, and stabbed the pig in the head, stopping it cold. The animal was on the ground kicking its hind legs in the air, desperately mustering the strength for another attack. Devereaux breathed hard, then he plunged the knife in the side of the boar. He twisted the knife, extracted it, and plunged again and again. The audibles coming from inside the barn were chilling but soon stopped.

Jack by now had no sense of what time it was. No idea if he killed the boar in the allotted 30 minutes. He just wanted to be somewhere reasonably comfortable and collapse in exhaustion. But this indefatigable gentleman of the Piedmont seized the moment. As Frank, Sheriff Brian, and the cousins were sitting on the cars drinking beer, the barn door kicked open, and out came Judge John P. Devereaux dragging a dead boar by the tail. The men all whooped and applauded, and one of the cousins emptied a whole beer on Devereaux's head.

"Frank, get me the hell out of here so I can go to bed until Monday," he whispered. Sore, exhausted, and partially traumatized, he thanked the rest of the clan and enjoyed a unanimous salute from them as he and Frank drove off the farm.

"That went about as well as anyone could have imagined, Judge. The boys are proud as peacocks of you. I could see it in their faces. Me especially, Judge. I don't think you'll ever have to prove yourself in any other way to us Kentuckians." Frank rambled on for another few minutes and then noticed that his passenger was dead fast asleep. As his car was buzzed passed the black iron gate at Bourbon Hill, he called for Geraldine to meet him and help him carry the Judge into the house and up to bed. Mrs. Devereaux was not pleased with McSherry when she clutched hold of her "half-dead" husband. "Don't try and explain yourselves to me, Frank," she scolded. "I didn't nurse him and fret over him for two months just to have history repeat itself."

"He's all right, Mrs. Devereaux, I assure you."

The two put the Judge in his bed and Frank took a not terribly subtle cue to exit the house for the evening. As he left the bedroom, the judge looked over and winked at him. It was a wink of complete approval and satisfaction toward the day's events. He was now one of the boys, and he commanded those boys—from now on, with total respect from the troops. Just two- or three-days' rest, and he would be good as new.

"I should skin you alive, Judge Devereaux, making me worry like this. I don't even want to know what you did with those mountain men. Just go to sleep, baby. I will give you a bath and wash these sheets tomorrow," Jeri said as she stroked his smiling face. She argued with herself for the rest of the evening, pondering why she was so impossibly attracted to such a willful and stubborn man.

Jack felt like the wealthy patrician in Ancient Rome. The one who just proved his manhood to the legion of which he was the head. It had been a very good day for Jack Devereaux. All of his exertions and risks had been worth it. As his wife persisted in her mental conflict, Devereaux was single-minded. He fell asleep with just one set of thoughts; how much more power he was accumulating.

Worlds were colliding in 21st Century rural Virginia. The world of the wealthy Devereauxs coupled with the ancient Appalachian culture of the McSherrys was under siege from the globalized and postmodern polluted masses of the large cities in America. Not so long ago, old money business interests in general were enough to secure the traditions of both patrician and hillbilly (I do not use the term pejoratively) in the conservative states of the union. But the technology monopolies had demanded a full-frontal rush into the space age and seemed to have no patience for a politics and culture, which refused to keep up with the resultant, deranged pace of change. These particular commercial interests do not want a society where Americans are paid high wages for specialized work, or any other work. So, they lean on politicians to import as much cheap labor as possible; people from all over the world descend upon places like northeastern Virginia—people of disparate backgrounds and cultures, ignorant of Virginian ways and inflaming the hostility of both rich landowner and middle-class farmer.

What truly lights the powder keg for a man like our Judge Devereaux is the increase in crime and disorder with these mass populations hovering far too close to the borders of his pastoral Piedmont paradise. Eventually, these urban masses become citizens and vote; thus, affecting the future legal and political power of Devereaux and like-minded friends and colleagues. Since this new order of things is anathema to Virginians of sensibility, they will employ a time-honored remedy to the presence of change and of outsiders: the secret society.

"I have to tell you, Judge. I hate Mondays," said an irritated Sergeant

McSherry to his boss.

"Just for curiosity's sake, why?" Devereaux inquired.

"Because it's the beginning of my several-day stretch at double duty. I go home too tired to mix it up with Mimi."

The judge gave a slight laugh, knowing firsthand how highly charged Mimi Charleville's appetites were, as well as her stamina. "I tell you what, Frank, when we find the piece of shit who paid to bump me off, I will give you an extra day off per week. Just make sure and assign me a substitute I can trust."

"Thank you, Judge," expressed a grateful McSherry. "By the way, did you hear back from the House Speaker? He looked agitated when I gave him your letter," Frank asked.

"No, but I ought to shortly. I may as well tell you now. There will be a vacancy soon on the Virginia Supreme Court. The Speaker will spearhead my appointment through the House."

"Why the Supreme Court? Won't you have to move to Richmond?"

"I'll keep a house there, but Bourbon Hill will be mine and Geraldine's regular home."

"Don't you have the power you want right now, Judge?"

"It's power enough for the time being. But I told you before, Frank, I don't like politicians. I don't trust them, hence our little game we play! In eight years, we could have a socialist legislature the way things are going in our country. I'm not about to bet my reappointment on any group of losers who are delusional enough to think they can make a difference in the world. No, the Supreme Court of Virginia is a lifetime appointment, Frank. Lifetime! Our little society can make all the difference we want with me on the Court for life." McSherry grinned with anticipation, again inspired and impressed by the machinations of his boss. "I expect to hear from our friend, the Speaker, by Wednesday. As for the State Senate, we will need to turn up the heat. I want Kelly Ann to take care of the Majority Leader personally.

He'll be putty in her hands, Frank."

"Yes, sir. Oh, I almost forgot, Judge. The Chief of the Bureau of Prisons signaled me that he's ready to do business."

"Well, well. What a way to begin the week!"

"How do you want me to get him started?"

"Just the way we discussed, Frank. This means we can dispense some hill country justice around here sooner than we thought."

Wednesday came and went, but neither McSherry nor Judge Devereaux heard a peep from the Virginia House Speaker. The judge was perturbed at having to wait on his extortion victim, but he had a sixth sense about these kinds of nefarious dealings. Without a doubt, he thought, the Speaker will cooperate but is holding out at the last minute for something by which he can save face. After all, he is a man of power too. Devereaux finished a brief one-day trial and went home to Geraldine and to some home cooking. He had a cocktail with his parents, where no conversation of import took place.

Mary Jane arrived just after the drinks and Jeri came down, and the five enjoyed a dinner of baby pheasant and beef tenderloin. Mary Jane had remained at the estate per Jack's request, and there was no place in the world at the moment that the Devereauxs, minus Courtney, would rather be than the illustrious Bourbon Hill dining room.

Jack might, by then, have been the undisputed Master of the House, but he had the foresight to insist that his father continue to occupy the seat at the head of the table. In fact, Thomas had asked the judge to trade seats so he could sit next to his wife. Jack saw right through it; it was a test question, one he passed thoroughly. "Pop, there is only one head of our family," he had said with his hand firmly and affectionately upon his father's shoulder.

During coffee and dessert, Corrine and Thomas informed the youngsters that they would be taking a European cruise beginning the following week and be gone for two months. "Oh, that's wonderful," declared Geraldine. "I've only ever been to the Caribbean. You'll have to send me videos and photos every day!"

Just then, the judge's cell phone rang. It was McSherry. "Let me take this outside, folks, my apologies."

Geraldine and Mary Jane fawned all over Corrine about their impending trip as Jack went out to the patio.

"I know who the bagman is," said McSherry.

"Is this what I think it is, Frank?"

"You better believe it, Judge. There is no doubt who paid the gunman to kill you."

Devereaux listened almost dispassionately to Frank's news. "Pick him up tomorrow morning and have him in my chambers at 2 p.m."

"With all due respect, Judge, shouldn't we have him locked up in county jail?"

"No, Frank. I don't want him arrested yet. Not until I've heard some answers."

"You don't believe he's an immediate threat?" Frank asked.

"My brother-in-law, Mr. Mansfield, doesn't have the balls to hit me again. I don't think he had the balls to do it in the first place, at least of his own accord."

"But Judge, all the evidence points to him paying off the shooter," Frank insisted.

"I'm afraid someone else put him up to it, I'm certain. But I have to dress him down, face to face, to prove it."

"Okay, sir, he and I will be in your chambers tomorrow at 2 p.m."

"Very good. And Frank, make the drive up here unpleasant for him." Jack hung up and returned to the dinner table with an easy smile. Thomas grilled him about the phone call.

Ordinarily, Jack would blow his father's concerns off, resenting the interference and control. But he had become increasingly tolerant of Thomas in every respect. Handing over a vast family estate to a young man of 36 tends to produce loyalty, even where little had previously existed. "Well, Pop. I may as well tell everyone. I'm being considered for a State Supreme Court appointment."

"Isn't that a lifetime appointment?" asked Mary Jane.

"Yes indeed," Jack replied.

"Is the job in Richmond, Jack? Would we have to move?" Jeri inquired.

"No, I would keep a house there for the court session and commute back here on weekends and the off season, which is surprisingly long," Jack explained. The ladies presented a toast, and Corrine blew Jack a kiss from across the table. Thomas, however, just sat quietly and ate his dessert. He had been around long enough to know that things were going a little too well for his son lately. And moving unusually fast. Not that he had begun to regret giving Jack Bourbon Hill, but his mind and his gut told him emphatically that Jack was not playing by the rules.

As Sergeant McSherry drove to Charlottesville to retrieve his suspect, he was shaking his head in amazement. Since the judge's shooting, he and his cohorts in state and local law enforcement had done their investigation by process of elimination of all people close to Devereaux, who had means and opportunity. Neither evidence nor speculation could provide a believable motive for the attempted murder, making their task more daunting. When Frank began to examine the bank records of certain individuals, he was stunned to find that a cash withdrawal of $250,000 had been made by none other than Mr. Timothy Mansfield one week prior to the shooting. Clinching the case was the fact that the deceased shooter, Randy Westover, was a part-time stable hand at the Mansfield Farm who cleaned the stables and turned out the horses for the Mansfields, a position he was hired to take over a year ago.

"This is amateur hour on steroids, Judge," McSherry had told Devereaux on last night's phone call. He couldn't believe how dumb Mansfield was and how lucky they all were. The veteran detective's instincts were gnawing at him to arrest Timothy Mansfield on the spot, drive him to the Sheriff's office, and interrogate him. But he followed Judge Devereaux's orders to the letter. He arrived at the Mansfield estate, drove through an open gate, and loudly and aggressively knocked on the front door.

"State Police, I need to see Mr. Timothy Mansfield," Frank barked as a young woman opened the door of the mansion house.

"I'm Timothy Mansfield," said a voice from the foyer. As he appeared, McSherry jammed him against the wall, frisking him, and placing him in handcuffs.

"I'm his wife, Courtney," said the woman at the door. "What is the meaning of this?" Alas, Courtney was Courtney, whether in a crisis or just for fun. Her hateful stare and acid tongue were on full display.

"Ma'am, your husband is wanted for questioning in felony illegal payoffs and money laundering." McSherry was still acting under the judge's instructions that nobody be privy to his knowledge that Mansfield ordered and paid for his shooting.

"You can't come in here like this, get out!" screamed Courtney as she shoved McSherry with both her hands. Frank grabbed her by the back of the hair and took her to the ground.

"I've broken people's wrists for doing less to me, Mrs. Mansfield. The only reason I don't pinch you right now for assault of a peace officer is...Well, you know the reason. Now shut your fucking pie hole and stop interfering with police business!"

"I'm calling the lawyer now, honey," said a mouthy but temporarily defeated Courtney. "Where are you taking him?"

"Warrenton, Sheriff's Office."

"You have him home by tonight or I will make trouble for you," Courtney

Mansfield threatened. McSherry just shook his head as he walked Timothy down the stairs and into the SUV.

He could hear the young Devereaux daughter cursing under her breath. "I must say, you have a foul-mouthed uppity bitch for a wife, Mansfield. I almost feel sorry you," said McSherry as he sucker-punched Timothy in his face. The two drove off the property and back onto Route 29, north toward Warrenton. Mansfield began to show emotion, for he had no clue what circumstances he was dealing with. As the car approached a stop light, McSherry punched him again, then again. Handcuffed and spitting blood from his mouth, Mansfield began to shake uncontrollably. Knowing he was guilty of the payoff, he wanted to burst into tears and beg Detective McSherry for leniency. But somehow, this mouse of a man who regularly let his wife use and abuse him found some inner strength at that very moment and was determined not to let McSherry or anyone else see him break down.

He knew, or so he thought, that his lawyer would be waiting for him at the Fauquier County Sheriff's Office and would soon secure his release. So, the young man who Judge Devereaux once had felt sorry for decided to be stoic for the remainder of the painful trip. McSherry parked behind the courthouse in Warrenton, away from cameras or bystanders. He opened the passenger door and let Mansfield have it. It only took seconds for his ribs to be bruised and jaw and cheekbones to be knotted. Now, Mansfield was in a right and proper condition for a private meeting with the judge.

As he and McSherry exited the elevator and walked into Devereaux's chambers, it was apparent that all the staff had been sent home early that day. Frank walked them into the judge's office where Devereaux sat behind his desk with his black robe on. As Frank took off his handcuffs, Mansfield sat down and began sobbing like a child. The judge and McSherry sat quietly with their arms folded. As Mansfield looked up after minutes of blubbering, he caught Devereaux's cold stare. Then he cried some more.

"Relax, Tim," ordered the judge. "We both know why you're here."

"I-I-I didn't want to do it, Jack, I promise you."

"Shut up, Mansfield," Frank said as he slammed his fist into the miserable man's knee.

"Frank, would you be so kind as to leave us alone for a few minutes?"

"Certainly, Judge." Frank walked out and shut the door. Mansfield continued sobbing and Devereaux walked over to his sideboard and poured his brother-in-law a scotch.

"At the risk of stating the obvious, you're in a heap of trouble, Tim," said the judge coldly as he sat down, putting Mansfield's drink on the desk. "I'm going to speak for a minute. Do not interrupt me! Afterwards, you will answer some questions. If all goes well, you will leave this courthouse with your health and your freedom. Do we understand each other?"

"Yes, yes, Jack."

"Judge! My friend. Judge, to you, from now on."

The disturbed victim drank his whiskey fast and nodded, "Yes, Judge."

"Good. Now, there is no use denying that you paid a low-life, drug-dealing ranch hand $250,000 to have me killed. We have you dead to rights. The only reason you are breathing is that I know you weren't acting alone. Hell, this wasn't even your idea, was it, Tim?" Devereaux stood up and refilled Mansfield's scotch glass, and the guilty man eventually regained some composure.

"I will do or say whatever you want, Judge."

"Who put you up to this?"

Mansfield went silent, his anxiety spiking. Despite two strong scotches, his shaking returned. Devereaux leaned over his side of the desk, knowing he had his victim in a vice grip. He also knew the answer to the question he was asking. "Who put you up to this, Tim?"

"Please, Judge. I assure you that there will not be a further attempt. They-they realize they made a mistake. You're...you're safe, Judge, I promise," stuttered Mansfield. The poor man was grasping at straws, desperately not wanting to reveal his accomplice. But having Devereaux inches from his face holding all the cards, this was the most terrifying experience of his life. For just a few moments, hapless and privileged Timothy Mansfield could not decide which was worse—answering the judge's question, or suffering at the hands of his henchman.

A third scotch was given to Mansfield, and as he began to calm, his mind delivered him a horrifying revelation. Judge Devereaux knew who his accomplice was, and he was toying with him. Eerie and mystical silence overtook the room as both men knew the answer to everything being discussed. "I want to hear it from you, Tim. Who told you to have me killed?"

Mansfield gave a painful and lengthy answer to the terrifying question. Devereaux then texted McSherry who entered the office and shut the door. The Detective Sergeant was made privy to the details and was then directed to allow Mansfield to first clean himself up, then take him on the 90-minute drive back to his Charlottesville farm.

The judge, relying chiefly on his own judgment, chose to believe Mansfield's story. The person in question was freaked out, almost remorseful when the assassination attempt failed. Since his brother-in-law was himself no threat, the shooter dead, and the accomplice pacified, Devereaux decided that very afternoon that no public or legal action would be taken regarding this affair. Any potential punishments and retributions would be meted out down the road. For the foreseeable future, he and McSherry would be tight with this secret, allowing only themselves and the guilty parties to know the truth. McSherry would lean on the county sheriff to sideline the investigation pending new evidence. Evidence which might never be presented.

McSherry dropped Mansfield at his gate. "Walk the rest of the way up to your house and tell your wife you've been cleared of all charges. Got it?"

"Yes, Detective," said a much-haunted Timothy Mansfield.

"And remember, we'll be watching you." Those words and an icy stare from a hard face with dark sunglasses were more than sufficient to mollify Mansfield into submission. As Frank drove off the estate, his phone rang.

"Is he still good and scared, Frank?"

"Yes, sir. He got the message and then some," Frank replied.

"Good, now we relax with this distraction for now and concentrate on our mission," directed a very purposeful Judge Devereaux. "The girlfriend, Natalie. Has she provided you with anything useful?"

"No, Judge, despite all that 'H' I have been supplying her. I don't think she knows anything frankly."

"Well, then," said the Judge. "Have her released into a rehab program. This may be one who deserves a second chance."

Why would Devereaux have McSherry supply drugs to an obvious addict only to order her release after the fact? Alarmingly, character is a difficult thing to measure, particularly if your goal is measuring a man's constancy. And we know what Emerson said about constancy! Devereaux may well have felt empathy for this girl. Who knows what ideas and motivations brewed inside the head of this multidimensional figure? One thing for sure is that the better part of wisdom suggests that he do something magnanimous for the only witness to his attempted murder. In this instance, compassion was the handmaiden of control.

Anyway, the judge was now in position to throw all of his attention to the task at hand, to secure his appointment to the State Supreme Court. With a lifetime judicial appointment on the highest court in the Commonwealth of Virginia, the Machiavellian power moves available to Devereaux were immeasurable. The Secret Society he envisioned and lusted after would necessarily come to concreteness. But would he and his fellows get away with it for long? Would this *Star Chamber* take on a life of its own and morph into something not even the judge could control?

VOLUME TWO

"There are but two powers: the sword and the mind."

— NAPOLEON BONAPARTE

CHAPTER I

Two Years Hence

Judge Jack Devereaux was now 38 years old. As his parents aged, he became the indisputable Lord of the Manor at Bourbon Hill and began increasingly to be looked upon as the head of the family. Mrs. Corrine Devereaux, when she and her husband were not traveling, spent her time in the impossibly well-manicured gardens of the estate and doted on her daughter-in-law, Geraldine. The two women had grown exceptionally close, making up for the lackluster parenting Jeri received from her divorced and sometimes bitter parents. Mr. Thomas Devereaux retired from law practice and spent his time playing golf at the most exclusive country club in Virginia. He continued to enjoy moving his considerable fortune around and giving his son legal advice, solicited or otherwise.

The judge had everything a man not even 40 could imagine, and then some. But despite his general contentment, he was raging internally due to a large slice of his plans having been recently curtailed. For he was passed over in the impending appointment to the Virginia Supreme Court, despite his sophisticated extortive efforts. As mentioned previously, politics is an unstable art, and notwithstanding overwhelming support in the House of Delegates (the Speaker especially), the very compromised Senate Majority Leader who had easily succumbed to the charms of Devereaux's top working girl resigned his seat due to campaign finance improprieties. A special election brought in a leader opposed to Devereaux and his friends and gave the Supreme Court seat to another man. It would be another six years before he would have to campaign behind the scenes for his reappointment to his current position as Circuit Court Judge. Depending on the political climate in the state and in the legislature, Devereaux could not control the outcome. This incensed him.

"My fate as a professional will fall to a bunch of two-bit hack politicians," constituted much of Jack's and Geraldine's pillow talk. It dominated their conversation one Friday evening.

"Goodness, Jack! You just made me feel a passion I haven't felt since you were shot. You must have some pinned up...something or other."

"Try pinned up rage, Jeri." Jack let down his guard, which was unusual for him. "It's ever since they turned me down for the State Supreme Court. You don't know how I lusted after that position."

"Jack, we're rich, we're young, and we're healthy. Isn't that enough to be happy?"

"Jeri, I am deliriously happy with our life together, our home, everything. But a man needs his vocational life, his purpose."

"And you're a distinguished lawyer and judge, honey."

"Listen, Jeri, I'm going try and explain this to you. That Supreme Court position was for a lifetime appointment. That meant no more scrutiny or political ass-kissing ever, period. In six years, my reappointment process begins, which means going to the Capitol, glad-handing, backslapping, and making promises to people I neither like nor respect. Just the idea of it all is intolerably demeaning."

Geraldine grabbed Jack's head and put it on her stomach. She began stroking his hair. "What is it you really want, sugar?"

"Don't think any less of me when I tell you, promise?"

"Of course, baby, what is it?"

"I will not stop until I have the power I want, power with no accountability to anyone but myself, excepting you and my inner sanctum." Jeri didn't respond right away, and the couple lie still for a few minutes, holding each other.

"How much power is enough for you, Jack?" Jeri asked in a more serious tone.

"I can't say, sweetheart. I don't even know myself how much is enough. I suppose I'll know it when I have it." Jack put his face in Jeri's face. Their eyes locked, their noses rubbed, and they could smell each other's breath. Then they kissed intensely for a few minutes but stopped short of another round. It was almost time to sleep. "All I know is Alexander Hamilton was right when he said he hated democracy."

"Careful, honey, Hamilton was killed in a duel," said Jeri, now more playful.

"Ha-ha, no worries. First, I contend that I'm a better shot than he was. Secondly, I have McSherry watching my back." Jeri sported a look of concern on her face at that moment but didn't let her husband see it. She was content with the discussion on the whole, however, for she knew that this rare bout of candor would not be easily or often repeated.

"Goodnight, baby," Jeri said. "You know, you are charming and clever enough to win over whoever you need." Jack smiled and kissed his wife and turned the light out. He would fall asleep with this one thought: that he shouldn't have to win people over anymore. He and he alone should dictate the terms of his office. Fortunately for him, that aforementioned Secret Society was becoming operational. There would be no regard for the democratic process in his next series of maneuvers.

Judge Devereaux didn't know it yet, but not becoming a Virginia Supreme Court Justice was a blessing in disguise. Things were being set in motion that no one could yet fully comprehend. When they would come to fruition, lives would never be the same. And some lives would cease to be. The Chief of the State Bureau of Prisons was about to prove himself indispensable to Devereaux and the boys. He was one on the list who did not require blackmail or other threats. Cash payments and VIP access to Devereaux's hookers motivated him right into the game. And it took no time at all for him to cough up some fresh victims for the Kentucky Gauntlet. The Kentuckians had built a fence around three sides of the property, the back acreage descending down a hill into dense woods. A creek separated the back portions, going further downhill which bordered another creek and into a fierce embankment, separating their land from their closest neighbor. It was truly a remote setting. Nobody could stumble in on any McSherry antics by accident. It was also impossible to hear any pronounced noises emanating from the farm, save a gunshot or two. Yes, Northwestern Fauquier County was certainly Gauntlet-friendly turf, a perfect destination for those in need of backwoods justice. Judge Devereaux had man-sized plans for this farm and its residents, who would mete out cruel and unusual punishment to some of the most deserving people.

Three gangsters from Northern Virginia had been occupying cells in the Fairfax County jail after murdering a rival gang member during a botched drug deal. They were all in the country illegally and should have been deported to their country of origin to do serious jail time there. The Governor's office had different plans and wanted them tried in Virginia. "Well, Frank, it seems that the new Governor is as dumb as the previous one," barked the judge in his office. "Prison overcrowding is a problem, Frank. The solution lies in two remedies: deport the illegals and stop locking people up for small-time drug use. It's a foolish drain on our system and its resources."

"Just one more reason why us cops hate politicians, Judge," Frank replied.

"Well, Frank, once our big thing is fully up and running, cops all over this state will be taking their orders from us, instead of politicians. Are the prisoners ready yet?"

"Yes, Judge. They're being driven to the courthouse now."

The judge shot Frank a sinister grin as he called his wife. "Hi, Jeri, tell everyone I won't be home for dinner. Late depositions going on here at the office." Jeri was in an ecstatic trance from the massage and full day spa treatment she had just received. Devereaux could have confessed to an orgy of call girls, and it might not have even registered. She told her husband she looked forward to seeing him later that night and then sank into the couch, listening to classical music. Jeri was asleep within seconds.

"You're coming to this one, aren't you, Judge?"

"Wouldn't miss it for the world."

Two hours later, the men entered McSherry's SUV with three handcuffed prisoners. The judge then called the Prison's Chief, thanked him for the delivery, and in coded language urged him to check his bank account the next morning. Frank drove fast to the farm in order to do the impending business before dark.

When they arrived, the cousins were lined up and waiting. Frank uncuffed the two underlings, leaving the gang leader bound as he led the man to a dark thicket of wood down the hill from the barn. "No Gauntlet today, fellows," shouted Devereaux. "These clowns aren't worthy. Just execute sentence, with prejudice. The prisoners spoke almost no English, but they sensed that something bad was about to happen. The two underlings ran like lightning back toward the truck. One of the cousins picked up a rifle and shot both men in their hips. Writhing and moaning, the condemned young men watched in horror as the other two cousins fell upon them, swinging their tomahawks, splitting their skulls down to the neck and killing them instantly.

Before Devereaux could say, "Justice served," he saw Frank walking back past the barn toward the boys and the dead men. "Where's the other scum-bag, Frank?"

"Handcuffed to a tree down in the bogs."

"And his punishment? Shouldn't he get worse than his hirelings?"

"Absolutely, sir. See that Rottweiler on the far side of the barn door?"

The judge gazed over to where Frank was pointing and at the German guard dog, muscular and elegant, who must have been 130 pounds or more, standing cold still as though discipline had been bred into him from birth. One of the cousins whistled at a deafening pitch and the dog took off run-ning down the hill. It disappeared into a dense fog that had suddenly risen out of nowhere. Frank took out a pint of whiskey, and they all passed it around. Just as Judge Devereaux took his swig, the crisp fall air was filled with the desperate screams of the gang leader. Frank went down to fetch the body as the dog with blood dripping from his teeth did a light jog over to the cousins, who petted and fawned all over their prized assassin. The fog began to thicken to the point where the McSherrys had to switch on the built-in flashlights on their rifles.

Devereaux and the McSherry cousins exchanged small talk as Frank emerged from the cloud cover and mist, dragging a closed-up body bag. As he and Devereaux locked eyes, Frank dissuaded him from looking at the dead man. They all had another drink and fed the Rottweiler, as the cousins took charge of disposal of the remains. Frank went inside to wash up and remove his utility clothes. As he burned them in a fire pit outside, the fog lifted with a similar rapidity as it formed. Devereaux had mixed emotions as he and Frank drove back to the courthouse. Of course, he was satisfied with the dispensation of Justice that ominous afternoon. But his stomach grew weak when he imagined himself, or any other man, trying to fight that Rottweiler instead of the wild boar he had killed with great dif-ficulty. Neither he nor Sergeant McSherry felt any sympathy for their three victims, but the judge was very happy to have his Gauntlet run behind him, for the McSherry clan seemed to be achieving new heights in creativity and cruelty in their rituals.

When the judge came home to Bourbon Hill, the large parlor and the dining room were empty. Geraldine had kept his dinner warm on a silver tray. He sat down immediately and began to eat. Halfway through his meal, he heard a dog bark in the far distance. His stomach knotted up again, he drank his wine but left a good part of his supper untouched. The dog continued to bark as the judge drank another glass of wine, then went upstairs to Geraldine. A hot shower and a comfortable robe prepared him for light conservation and affection with Mrs. Devereaux. It was sufficiently good that night, and the judge fell into a deep sleep, dispensing with any thoughts that might continue to disturb a man.

The next day, Devereaux was taking a recess from court when the Chief Judge phoned him. The conversation was solely about a planned judicial overhaul bill the legislature would take up in January at the beginning of the session. At the top of their list was a phasing out of lifetime appointments for State Supreme Court Justices. This was in direct response to the Chief of the that court, who was 91 years old and not altogether lucid. Additionally, Courts of Appeal Judges and Circuit Judges would face reappointment every six years instead of the current nine years. Normally, this would tend to subject the judges to more political oversight. A most lovely little amendment was added, however. And were this overhaul bill to pass, it would remove as much politics from the appointment process as possible. The preferred proposal, according to the Chief Judge, would be to have the full legislature (required by law) rubber stamp all judges recommended by the Delegates and Senators from their respective circuits.

In Devereaux's case, the Delegates and Senators representing Fauquier, Culpeper, and Rappahannock counties were all of Judge Devereaux's stripe on the issues of the day and people who had received generous donations from his father. This all but accidental gift played right into Devereaux's hands. Certainly, the bill would contain a provision that all judges could be denied reappointment by the full legislature for serious allegations of illegality, impropriety or unfitness for the position. But that was not a risk for him. Also, removing the lifetime appointment made remaining a circuit court judge more desirable due to the enforcement power of that level of court. "Thanks for the rundown, Fred," said Devereaux as he hung up the phone. "Well, it appears circumstance is not trying to piss on me this time," he said to himself.

According to the Chief Judge, the new Senate leader was the impetus behind the idea; the same leader who intentionally passed Devereaux up for the Supreme Court, an irony not lost on our young judge. With the Speaker of the House corralled like a bull, this new bill should be a cinch.

Leaving nothing to chance, those legislators already in the Judge's vice grip would be given new prioritized orders to support the judicial reform legislation. And the masterful performance of Devereaux's ladies on their extra randy targets would certainly yield more victims to the judge's designs. He was now virtually unconcerned with maintaining his power and position as a judge. No sooner had Jack assumed his confident air than he was called back into court to read a guilty verdict in a business investor blackmailing case. Of course, the defendants were to receive the maximum sentence the following week.

Courtney Mansfield was bored to tears at her ranch. It was a supreme autumn day in the Piedmont. Almost 70 degrees with no clouds in an overarching blue sky, the climate accentuated the majestic and historic Blue Ridge Mountains. Courtney decided to leave her husband at home and go for a drive. Sporting a fashionable purple sweater, tight jeans, and boots, her fabulous golden hair pulled back in a ponytail, she turned every head as she eased her red Mercedes Convertible through the main street in

Charlottesville. Stopping at a wine and cheese store, she double parked and went inside to purchase something delicious from one of her best friends, the owner. The proprietor recommended a South African Sauvignon Blanc.

"This will do nicely, Sarah, thanks," said Courtney as she hugged and kissed her friend. The two young ladies had gone to private school together since they were seven. Sarah's mother had been almost a second mother to Courtney (or at least an affectionate aunt). Just then, Sarah's mother emerged from the storeroom. Courtney hadn't seen her in a couple of years since Mrs. Palmer moved to Florida. As the older woman called to her with arms stretched out, Courtney almost dropped the wine bottle in surprise and delight. She threw herself into Mrs. Palmer's arms, the two women hugging firmly.

"Oh, what a peach you are, sweetheart," said Mrs. Palmer as she placed her hands on Courtney's cheeks.

It appears that Mrs. Mansfield was capable of affection after all, but the evidence suggests it was reserved for a select few. Courtney kissed Sarah Palmer goodbye and thanked her for the wine. She then repeated the passionate embrace with Mrs. Palmer and gladly accepted her gracious invitation to visit her in Florida. With that, she mounted her Mercedes, barely missing a police officer on patrol—one who would have, in all likelihood, given her a ticket for double parking. As she stopped at the final stoplight before the town street turned into a rural state highway, Courtney uncorked the wine and poured half of it into a thermos. As she sped down the narrow road, she drove with one hand and sipped the excellent wine with her other. Twists, turns, and constant ups and downs on the mountain presented a dream outing for the car and wine enthusiast.

No one could possibly know what Courtney Mansfield had on her mind just before she lost control of her luxurious automobile and tumbled down into a gorge on the left side of the road.

CHAPTER 2

Later that afternoon, Judge Devereaux drove to Charlottesville to meet with a psychiatrist. This he did at the not so gentle request of his wife. Geraldine had been both worried and weary of his increasing night terrors. For several weeks, Jack had woken up in the middle of the night or early in the morning sweating and short of breath. Jeri had heard him mutter the same words each time: "Stop, stop the screams. No! They deserve what they get. They deserve it, I'll keep giving it to them. Damn those screams!"

Jack walked into the office of the only therapist on earth he trusted. "Sit down, little brother, and breathe deeply," said a genuinely loving but fiercely professional Dr. Mary Jane Devereaux. Jack breathed as directed but began to sweat and grew totally out of character at his inability to control his nerves. "Despite the obvious personal connection, I'm going to ask you a question," insisted Mary Jane. "What is your name and what do you do?"

"My name is Judge John Devereaux. I am a man who makes other men scream. If that's not enough, I also run the criminal justice system in Virginia." The judge then paused, staring hauntingly at his sister/therapist. Mary Jane sat in her command chair blindsided, unsure of how to respond to the two statements. The first one suggested to her that Jack was involved in activity which greatly troubled him. But the second one suggested a man with delusions of grandeur.

After minutes of silence and disconcerting body language, Mary Jane chose to address the second statement. "Why would you say that you control the entire justice system in the Commonwealth of Virginia? You are only one of hundreds of public officials," she asserted.

"Oh, my dear," sighed Jack. "A secret, very small, and unaccountable society runs Virginia, Mary Jane. We decide how justice is meted out, keep elected officials in line, and get rid of undesirables." Devereaux was both confident and comfortable confessing his demons to his sister. She was not only beloved to him but was by law forbidden, as a psychiatrist, to divulge anything he said to her. "It sounds like a mere boast on my part, Mary Jane, but I'm telling you this piece of things because I want you to understand how serious and consequential my power is."

Not knowing how to respond to this epiphany, Dr. Devereaux shifted gears and honed in on his "scream" comment. "How do you make other men scream, Jack? I'm assuming it's a metaphor for putting people in prison; harsh sentences and the like?"

"I wish it was simply a metaphor," the judge retorted. "I am responsible for ordering and implementing horrific punishments on many terrible, awful people."

"I trust that makes you feel good, Jack," she said.

"It does, believe me, it does. In every conceivable way."

"Then what's the problem?"

"I can't stand the screams anymore."

Mary Jane looked confused. She was confused. "Tell me exactly what screams from what people are bothering you?"

Jack leaned forward and spent the rest of the session telling his sister all about the McSherry clan and the farm. He enjoyed thoroughly trying to impress her that he was willing to get his own hands dirty, participating in the sentences carried out there. But Mary Jane remained stoic, focusing on what Jack had admitted as the conflict within him. "You said you enjoyed participating in this clandestine, certainly illegal, punishment of criminals. But you can no longer tolerate the reactions of your victims to your violent actions."

"Victims?"

"What would you call them, Jack? Sure, they may be lowlifes who deserve justice, but they are prisoners in your clutches, and I assume those of your cohorts. So, in a way they are victims of your violence."

"And that is the way it has to be," Jack said. "I seek no redemption from you or anyone else. I just want help with the screams. I need to remain effective and also to be able to live with myself." Devereaux got out of his chair and toweringly approached his sister. Dropping down to one knee, he put his hands on her face tightly and looked piercingly into her eyes. "I am counting on you to help me with this."

"I will try, little brother. Our session is over for today. See me in three days and we will continue."

Jack gently kissed Mary Jane on her forehead. As he gathered his coat and briefcase, Mary Jane checked her cell phone for messages from other patients. "Oh, my goodness, no! No!" She called Jack back into the office.

"What is it, sis?"

"That was Mom. Courtney has been in an awful car accident. She's in a coma."

"So much for *my* problem, then," Jack muttered to himself. Even the judge was surprised at the callousness of his own mumblings. "Does she want us to do something?" he asked. "My phone is in the truck. She's probably trying to reach me now."

"Obviously she doesn't know you're here, Jack. We have to go to University Hospital here in Charlottesville. Maybe..."

"One of Frank's men is outside in a squad car. I'll have him escort us to the hospital." Mary Jane locked up her office and headed out to Jack's vehicle. "You drive," Devereaux suggested. "I have a mountain of phone messages."

As his sister put a lead foot on the SUV, Jack texted Jeri, who had gone to the hospital. Then he called McSherry. "Frank, I just now got your message. When did it happen? Other cars involved? Send two of your guys to the hospital quickly, will you? My parents are there already."

"What happened, Jack?" inquired Mary Jane as she drove recklessly towards the hospital.

"Near as McSherry could tell, she was driving by herself, drinking wine but not drunk. She was on Deep Gorge Road."

"Oh my, that's dangerous, Jack. Why would she drive there?"

"For the thrill of it, I'm sure. That Mercedes of hers is a hot, fast piece of work."

Mary Jane started crying. "I know we've had a lifetime of angst, she and I. But for her to end up this way..."

"Hush, sister, save it for when we know something more. People go in and out of comas all the time. UVA has the best doctors around." As they pulled up to the hospital, Mary Jane double parked, and their father, who was outside waiting for them, broke the news.

"Your sister died 10 minutes ago," said Thomas, holding back tears. Mary Jane flung herself into Thomas's arms.

"Where's Mom?" asked Jack.

"She, Geraldine, and Timothy are in with the nurses. Neither of them is in very good shape."

"That's to be expected, Pop."

"Son, walk with me privately." Jack nodded to Mary Jane, who then ran inside the hospital. "I know we are dealing with a car accident on a dangerous highway. And I know Courtney liked to drink and drive fast. But I am also superstitious. Someone tried to kill you, Jack. And now your sister is dead."

"What are you asking, Pop?"

"I'm asking you, son, to use of all your powers and authority and investigate this accident as though your life depended on it. I want to know without a doubt that this was an unfortunate accident. Are we clear?"

"Yes, Pop. We're clear. Frank is still out at the crash site; I'll make sure he heads the investigation. And he reports directly to me."

"Thank you, son." Thomas put his arm around Jack, and the two walked and talked some more. "This is pain like you can't even imagine, boy. The way I'm feeling right now, I would counsel you and Geraldine never to have children. It's far worse to have had them and lose them." Thomas's eyes welled up with tears and he became more vulnerable than the judge had ever seen him. "A beautiful young girl, full of life, so full of piss and vinegar. And I outlive her! It's all wrong, son. All so very wrong."

The judge had no tears in his eyes, but he was not unmoved. He was shaken up by his father's understandable emotions. More so by his showing them in such a pronounced fashion. He was sad for both of his parents, who would suffer from this tragedy for the rest of their days. The thought of never seeing Courtney again had not registered in his mind. At least not yet. He gently walked his father into the rooms where Courtney had laid. Thomas comforted Corrine, Jack and Geraldine comforted each other, and a very distraught Timothy Mansfield was comforted by his parents. The two clans then retreated to a lounge where they could all sit privately and drink coffee.

Paul and Maureen Mansfield had a family cemetery on their estate which dated back to the War of 1812. They politely offered that Courtney should be interred there. Ever the traditionalists, the Devereauxs assumed that all of them would be buried at the family parish, St. George's Episcopal Church in Markham. But Corrine and Thomas had seen the magnificent Mansfield cemetery many times. And the Mansfields' offer had warmed their hearts on this disastrous day. It was as if the two families had become one for the first time. It took no more than a few minutes for the Devereauxs to concur. "Yes," said Thomas. "That would be the best place for her."

Corrine and Mary Jane concurred, and Jack nodded his emotionless approval. Jack and Timothy had not exchanged pleasantries or barely looked at each other. They were privy to a secret that nobody else knew. The judge wanted like hell to get out of there and go home with Jeri. But he would stay as long as it took to have a brief and private conversation with his brother-in-law.

Astonishingly, the timid one rose from his seat and asked Jack to take a walk with him. Devereaux excused himself from the two families, grabbed another coffee, and went for that walk. When they were out of earshot, Timothy came right out and asked the question. "You told me emphatically on that awful day not too long ago that you were not going to make me a widower, Jack. I believed you. Now my wife is dead, in a car crash. You know what a good driver she was. Tell me you didn't do it."

"Do what, Tim?"

"You know very well what."

Jack reminded Timothy what had happened the last time he made him angry. "Now listen good, you pissant," he said. "You and your wife tried to have me popped. I should have killed you both, and I would have if such an action wouldn't have hurt all those good people back there," Devereaux said as he pointed back to the family lounge.

"Jack, you promised not to harm her when I guaranteed that she was pacified and remorseful for what she had done."

"And I kept that promise. This was an accident, and my officers will prove it shortly. Look, I'm sorry for your loss. But tread lightly with me, Tim. You have no idea what evil might come your way." Devereaux stopped walking and glared into Timothy's face. "I know it was you, Tim, you alone. Then you must have boasted about it to Courtney afterward. Tell me, did she approve or reproach you?" Mansfield's face could not have registered more horror had he seen a vampire. He began to shake and stutter. "You continue to exist only by my good graces, Tim. Should

I wake one morning in a particularly vengeful mood, then it's lights out for you, pal. Do we understand each other?"

Timothy was weak by nature, hence his everlasting propensity to be his wife's doormat. Every marriage that lasts, though, has a power behind it; a mysterious power which keeps it together. Weak, but not a complete fool, Mansfield understood the young lady with whom he fell in love and married. It was the combination of his love for Courtney and his need to wake up every day and be her husband, come what may, which rendered his leaving her an impossibility. The poor man settled for the mere crumbs of affection he was given. And despite all the hurt, that was enough for him. Now, he had her no more. In one long second, Mansfield's mind returned to the moment he told Courtney he was ridding the world of her detested brother. She had rewarded his unexpected efforts with passion and a very palpably felt respect. Alas, that respect and affection evaporated when Judge Devereaux survived the shooting.

When Jack and Timothy returned to the lounge and their families, Timothy was white as a sheet and sweating. He looked at his mother and cried. His parents got up to console him and then he collapsed from his awful exhaustion. Devastating sadness turned into a raw and frightful panic attack, and Timothy Mansfield was rushed into intensive care for observation. Jack now had his answer to the previous accusation.

As the family called for a nurse, the judge whisked Geraldine outside. "I can't stay in there any longer, honey," he said.

"Why are you so anxious, Jack?"

"I can't take any more tragic sadness and nervous breakdowns. I need whiskey now."

Geraldine didn't know how to respond. She knew her husband and his younger sister detested each other. But to leave the family at a moment like this seemed unthinkable.

"Go back inside and tell Pop I have to meet with the state police concerning the accident. He'll know what I'm talking about."

"But Jack..."

"Do like I say, sweetheart. Tell them we will see them back at Bourbon Hill tonight. And tell Mary Jane to stay with the folks and ride back with them."

"I should stay here too, Jack."

"No, you're coming with me."

Geraldine returned from her mission and got into the truck with the judge, who was talking on his phone. "Send the two officers behind me now back to the estate. Put some extra security around the Mansfields' place and meet me at Bourbon Hill in an hour. Thanks, Frank."

Devereaux drove to the nearest liquor store and came back out with a bottle of scotch. Geraldine knew the score and immediately took the driver's seat so Jack could drink a significant portion of the hooch on the 90-minute drive back home. "No talking, okay, Jeri?" he pleaded. "I just want your presence and this bottle."

Jeri smiled as Jack stroked her leg and then held her hand. He drank with the other hand after putting his phone in the glove box. He sensed that he was enjoying the last hour and a half of peace and quiet he would have for a while.

CHAPTER 3

Someone cut the brake lines in your sister's car, Judge," said Sergeant McSherry.

"Are you sure? I mean, hard evidence, Frank," Jack inquired.

"That's the thing. We have no hard evidence. The crash was so violent that it destroyed the whole brake system, along with most everything else."

"Then why do you think the lines were tampered with?"

"That's the reason I was there for so long, examining the track and skid marks. What I noticed was a seemingly endless pattern of zigzags. Rubber marks made by the front tires. In most crashes, these are accompanied by thick rubber marks made by the rear tires when the driver brakes frantically at the same time that they lose control of the steering. I couldn't find such rear tire marks except at the very beginning of the skids. She must have braked immediately after losing control, but then for almost a quarter mile there were no rear skid marks."

Jack Devereaux poured the rest of his scotch into a glass and gave it to Frank. The men sat in the empty parlor off the dining room at Bourbon Hill. Geraldine was asleep upstairs. "I didn't do it, in case you're wondering, Frank. I wasn't involved."

"I didn't think you were, Judge," Frank said as he knocked back his whiskey.

"You had every right, though. With her behind your murder attempt."

"It wasn't her idea, Frank."

"Come again?"

"Oh, she must have known about it, but Mansfield ordered the hit and paid for it on his own. He must have thought that, had it succeeded, he would have earned Courtney's love and admiration for the rest of their lives."

"But Judge, I was there in your chambers the day I brought Mansfield in. He told us the whole story."

"When you stepped out of the room, Frank, I leaned into him hard. I thought Courtney might have put him up to it, given that he's so weak. But reading his eyes and his face, I got a sixth sense that I was dealing with a desperate man. One who needed to prove himself."

"Prove himself to who, Judge?"

"To his wife, to himself. So, I forbade any action against Courtney and made Tim live with the fear and the guilt. Today at the hospital, my suspicions were confirmed. When I grilled him in private, he was sad and distraught over his wife. Then he had a panic attack and went into the ICU."

"What does this all mean, Judge? Are you saying..."

"Yes, Frank. I am saying that he tried to have me whacked in order to show his wife he was a man, that maybe then she would love him properly. When we interrogated him, though, he showed his true colors again and blamed Courtney for the whole thing."

"You don't think he had his wife killed, do you, Judge?"

"No, obviously not. She was his world, the reason behind all of his stupid meanderings. No, Frank. Tim didn't kill her. I didn't kill her, and she had no known enemies. It had to be a terrible accident."

The judge went to the wet bar for some more whiskey and kept himself and McSherry from drying out. "I promised my father I would take control of the investigation. Any other evidence or hunches on your part, Frank?"

"No, that about clears it for now. But if I were putting money on it, I still say the brakes were tampered with. Tell your father what you want, but I wouldn't completely forget this case, Judge."

"Duly noted, Frank. Duly noted."

At Devereaux's behest, Sergeant McSherry and the state police ruled Courtney's death an accident. Jack told his father the next evening at cocktails. "I wanted to talk to you privately, Pop. It was a terrible, terrible accident. No evidence of anything else. State police and the medical examiner ruled on it this afternoon. The doctors uncovered nothing but a small amount of alcohol in her system. She died of her crash injuries. Let's put this behind us, Pop. We have memorial services to plan."

Thomas just looked at his son with gratitude and drank far more than was his usual amount. He could not speak.

The scent of incest was solemn and gripping as it accented the timeless beauty of All Saints Episcopal Church in Albemarle County. On a hillside no more than five miles from Thomas Jefferson's Monticello, the old stone church presented itself as a mini cathedral. Smells, bells, pipes, and trumpets engulfed the congregants and mourners in this Anglican High Mass funeral service. The two-mile procession to the Mansfield estate took a painfully longer time than it should have, for the church was packed with people the Mansfields and the Devereauxs knew but had not seen in years. The kinds of people who only show up at tragedies and celebrations.

Courtney Devereaux Mansfield was laid to rest at her in-laws' family cemetery. Thomas and Corrine were overwhelmed by the honor guard supplied by their son. Frank McSherry and his subordinates in the state police were in full dress uniform, as were the sheriffs of Fauquier County, Albemarle County, and Sheriff Brian McSherry of Buchanan County. Deputies and troopers made a perimeter around the graveside service and escorted ladies back to their vehicles. Frank and Mimi were invited back to Bourbon Hill for another private devotional gathering honoring Courtney.

As the Devereaux motorcade passed through the black iron gate at

Bourbon Hill, not a word was uttered. All of the body language issued by any of the family members was instantly understood by everyone else. As they got out of their vehicles, the gate opened again for the rector of St. George's Church and his wife, who drove up to meet Thomas and Corrine.

It was cocktail hour once again at Bourbon Hill, and Corrine and Thomas required the spiritual comfort of their pastor and his wife. Mary Jane stayed in the larger parlor with them. Jack and Geraldine went to another part of the house at Jack's insistence. "Isn't it rude for us to not be with everyone now, Jack?" Geraldine inquired.

"A church service and a burial are quite enough religion for one day, honey. Don't you think?"

"I know how you feel, baby, but..."

"We have done our duty, Jeri. Time to get back to normal around here. Mom and Pop will never fully recover from what's happened, but we have to. For our own sanity. Agreed?"

"I guess I understand," said Jeri grudgingly.

"Meanwhile, we have to make Frank and Mimi feel at home."

"Ah, yes."

Geraldine had heard much about Miss Mimi Charleville but had never had an actual conversation with her. As the four of them sat down, Mimi was not about to risk saying anything that might make Devereaux look bad to his wife. So, Jeri did most of the talking. By the end of the two-hour long conversation, Mimi had convinced Jeri to join her the following week and look at some houses to buy as potential rental properties. Both Jack and Frank were relieved when the ladies exited the room for the kitchen with Mimi's laptop computer to look at homes.

As Devereaux started to rise from his chair, Frank motioned for him to sit. "You're always pouring me the best hooch, Judge. So, I brought a little treat with me from Kentucky." With that, McSherry went to the bar and poured some moonshine into two small glasses. He handed one to the judge.

As they drank, the two men winced and groaned, then coughed. "Damn that's good, what do you think, Judge?"

Devereaux cleared his throat, smiled, then cleared his throat again. Then he took out a handkerchief and wiped his forehead and his eyes. McSherry laughed, enjoying his boss being temporarily in his power. "That certainly is the strongest shit I've ever had," Jack said.

Just then, McSherry's cell phone rang. "It's Kelly Ann, sir."

"Put it on speaker," Jack said as he shut the door.

"Go ahead, honey," said Frank.

"The Attorney General is compromised. Got it?"

"Got it, sugar, well done." Frank hung up and looked at Devereaux. "The Attorney General of this Commonwealth is ours."

"Well, well, Frank. I know we imagined this, we planned it. But the extortion piece of our operation seems a bit too easy. What's the catch, Frank?"

"There is no catch, sir. We just keep doing our thing and stacking up casualties."

"You know what this means, though. The Attorney General *and* the Chief of the Bureau of Prisons in our clutches?"

"Yes, Judge, I know exactly what it means," said the grinning detective.

"Let's have another shot of that rot gut, Frank." The conspirators threw down the moonshine, coughing and sweating. "Time to put the Fairfax Plan into motion, Frank."

"Yes, sir."

"Call a meeting with the Attorney General, the Prison Chief, and Judge Bean of the Fairfax County Circuit Court."

"When and where, Judge?"

"Right here, a week from Monday, 12 p.m."

"I wish I was a fly on the wall for this meeting, Judge."

"I can tape it for you if you'd like, Frank." McSherry laughed devilishly. "I just can't wait to see all these gentlemen's faces when they realize they're in the same room together," laughed Judge Devereaux.

Dinner ensued, and the rector and his wife provided much needed consolation to Thomas and Corinne. As the evening wrapped, everyone realized his or her total exhaustion at the day's happenings. As Mary Jane and Corrine stayed inside, Thomas walked the church couple out to their car. Jack and Geraldine did the same for Frank and Mimi. Jeri gave Mimi a warm hug and told her how excited she was to be looking at properties with her.

Jack approved of this distraction, and he shook hands with McSherry. "Thank you for everything today, Frank. We are all very grateful to you."

"My pleasure, sir." The two shook hands again, not so much as colleagues but as friends. Mimi winked at Jack as she got into the car.

"You know, Jeri, it's only 10 p.m. Why don't we…"

"Oh no, you don't! I'm going to sleep for twelve hours," Jeri said emphatically.

Devereaux, too tired and drunk to argue, went to bed with her and slept. Eight and a half hours later, the judge stirred and opened one of the curtains. Geraldine gently awoke and noticed her husband with a fresh scent and mouthwash lying next to her, grinning ear to ear. She turned over on him and they had a tremendous time together.

As Jack began to plea with Jeri for an encore, there was a knock at the door. It was Mary Jane, asking if he and Jeri would like breakfast in bed. Before Jack could dismiss the offer, Geraldine yelled out, "Of course, that would be lovely!"

The judge was displeased at having to delay his second round, but he didn't show it. "What's gotten into her? I don't ever remember Mary Jane being this attentive. This is something Mom would do."

"I'm sure it's all about the recent family loss, honey. She's feeling sentimental. Just go with it."

"I can do that, darling," he said. Jack observed his sister curiously. She needed to be in her right mind during their next therapy session, for the judge would need to lean on her. He had phobias to surmount and secrets to share. Four days hence, he did.

"Getting back to the screams, Jack," Mary Jane directed during their session. She sensed that her brother was less interested in confession and atonement than he was at getting past something that had been bothering him to incapacitation. She did not want to know if he had been breaking any laws. She did not want him to confirm what she already suspected; that he was in some way involved with violence. That that violence had disturbed Jack, and he wanted her to treat him—not to reform, but to supply coping skills that would enhance his ability to carry out his misdeeds, whatever they may have been.

Jack, sensing almost everything Mary Jane was afraid of, took the reins. "In my capacity as a judge, I and some colleagues impose sentences on people that make them scream, let's just say for argument's sake, metaphorically. I choose to be present when some of these sentences are carried out. I cannot allow my cohorts to think me squeamish, you see."

"I see," said Mary Jane. "And if you have the respect of your...cohorts...do you have to continue being present at these...sentencings?"

"No, I don't have to be there at all, really. But I wish to reserve the right to be there at some of them. And when that happens, I cannot be allowed to suffer the details. Am I making sense, sis?"

"You are, but I need to clarify something. Something that may be a deal-breaker for me to continue helping you."

Devereaux, anticipating the next line of questions, preempted his sister. "Now, listen to me closely," Jack said in a calm and reassuring tone. "We do not harm innocent people. We protect them. We protect the prey from the predators, and that sometimes involves dishing out brutal treatment to the predators. I have never harmed any innocent people, and I never will."

Mary Jane was relieved, though she still wanted to skirt the issues of violence and illegalities. "I will continue to help you all I can, Jack. Your two matters are, I believe, inextricably linked. The secret society you mentioned and the 'details of your carrying out sentences on the predators in our midst' can be dealt with. But please try and answer all of the questions I pose to you in our next session as best you can—without telling me something that I cannot be allowed to hear. Agreed?" Jack smiled, never doubting his sister's ability and desire to assist him. "Come see me next Wednesday. Until then, I advise you not to participate in any 'screaming' activities."

"Good advice, sis, thanks!"

Devereaux left feeling better than when he began the day's session. And that was the whole point. A half a dozen gang bangers were being transferred from the Fairfax County jail to Warrenton. From Warrenton, they would go to the farm, and to their deaths. Jack would not be there. He would simply issue the orders to Frank and the other McSherrys. Within just a few months, scores of the worst of the worst offenders in Virginia jails would be methodically transferred to either the farm in Fauquier County or the new one in Buchanan County in southwestern Virginia, run by Frank's brother, Sheriff Brian McSherry.

Official papers and judicial forms would be provided, and at the proper subsequent moment, lost and destroyed. Bodies were disposed of where they could never be found. Yes, this was quite a society of scofflaw lawmen. If nobody talked, Judge Devereaux's operational fortress was all but impregnable.

CHAPTER 4

The judge returned to Bourbon Hill that evening expecting a light family dinner. His mother told him to retrieve Geraldine, who had been upstairs all afternoon. As he mounted the staircase and turned toward the master suite, he heard frustrated crying coming from the bathroom. It was Geraldine, in her underwear, frantically pulling out small clumps of her hair.

Devereaux rushed in and took hold of his wife's arms, leading her out to the sofa. She would not stop crying until Jack rocked them both back into the couch holding her tightly, gently kissing her head and caressing her cheeks. "Do you want to tell me what happened, Jeri?" he softly asked.

"It's stupid, I feel so stupid," she replied.

"Nonsense, tell me."

"I've been shedding hair all day—in the shower, in my brush and comb. It won't stop!" She grew more agitated. "It's all because of this new perm solution at Mr. Ralph's Salon. He talked me into trying it." Jeri wanted to tell her husband about the more likely reason for her hair shedding and mood swings but hesitated. "I went back there earlier today to complain and get my money back. Mr. Ralph said it's a normal side effect in the beginning, but it can't be. I'm losing my hair in droves! And then he told me that he never gives refunds, and as I got upset, he just giggled."

"Giggled?"

"Yes, he was giggling at my expense. I don't like to drop your name every time I have a problem, but I was so upset I started to tell him who you were, and then I could hear the two hair stylists in the back laughing too. The more I demanded a refund, the more Mr. Ralph giggled, and the women in the back said I was a half-breed," Jeri began to sob.

Jack squeezed her tightly again and held her face close to his. "Sweetheart, tell me everything they said."

"They said I was a half-breed and that I had no business being a client of their establishment. They said I was too fat." Jeri paused and looked at Jack. Tears kept streaming down her face as she continued. "I have never been so humiliated. I didn't want to give them any satisfaction, so I said this was not the last of it and stormed out. But as I started driving away, I burst into tears. Oh, Jack, why are people so unnecessarily cruel. I thought they were my friends."

"Hush, sweetie. Never you mind what people like that think. My dermatologist is a scalp specialist. She will take care of your hair shedding and treat the damage from the solution. Remember before we got married, you caught me freaking out about my grays? Dr. Walton took good care of me. It will all be okay quickly. Understood?" Jeri sniffed and nodded in the affirmative. "Here's the name and number. Go ahead and make the appointment and drop my name. I promise everything will be alright, honey," he said as he cupped her face and kissed her gently on the nose.

The next day, Geraldine enjoyed a soothing and reassuring appointment at the dermatologist. Afterwards, she went to see her doctor about the other thing. She was reassured on that score as well.

That afternoon, Mr. Ralph's Salon had two visitors. Noticing there were no customers in either the chairs or the waiting room, the judge went back to the front door and turned the open sign to closed. He then pulled the blinds and locked the door. Mr. Ralph and one of the stylists came out of the stockroom startled.

"Who are you gentlemen? And why are my blinds pulled?"

Frank McSherry glared at him and told him he was closed for the day. As the two frightened people glanced toward the telephone, Devereaux said, "I'm here for my refund."

"What refund?" Mr. Ralph inquired.

"Jeri Devereaux's refund. She's my wife!" The owner glanced at his phone again. "There's no need to call the police," Devereaux said. "Allow me to introduce you to the police." He pointed to McSherry. Just then, another stylist and what appeared to be a young assistant came out of the back room. "Which one of you insulted my wife and said she shouldn't be a client here?"

As the staff paused in abject terror, Frank cracked his knuckles and pulled back his jacket, displaying his gun and holster.

"Both these bitches said those horrible things to your wife," said the young assistant.

The stylists frantically accused the girl of lying. Devereaux asked her gently what was said.

"They said she was fat and had no business being our client. And this bitch called her a half-breed. I hate it here. They treat me like shit." The girl looked at Mr. Ralph, eyes like daggers, and then back at the two visitors. "I quit. Can I leave, Officer?"

Devereaux nodded and McSherry let the young girl leave. Frank locked the door and Devereaux said, "I'm telling you for the last time, I will have my refund now—four-hundred dollars."

Mr. Ralph amazingly mustered up a modicum of indignation. "You're the police—you have rules. You can't just come in here like this. I demand to know who your supervisor is," said a now hyperactive Mr. Ralph.

"You're looking at him, asshole," said Frank, pointing to the judge. Then Devereaux put a glove on his right hand and gut-punched Mr. Ralph. Before the man could catch his breath, the judge had him by the testicles and twisted with considerable strength. The unfortunate owner screamed bloody murder and begged Devereaux to let go so he could retrieve the cash from his register. Jack let go, and Mr. Ralph, now crying, sauntered over to the register and took out four-hundred dollars cash and gave it to Devereaux.

While that scene was unfolding, Frank had whisked the women to the stock room. Jack had been too busy with the owner to notice the women's screams coming from the back. As he placed the cash in his coat pocket, the judge waited for Frank to come out from the back room. As he emerged, Jack could hear the two hair stylists moaning in the rear.

"I'll be keeping my eye on you, Mr. Ralph," he said. "Making sure you run a respectable business. Oh, and Geraldine won't be coming back. Your loss, maggot!"

The men entered Frank's vehicle and drove away. "That sissy Mr. Ralph provided us with some harmonizing entertainment, Frank."

"Are you talking about his high-pitched screaming, Judge?"

"Precisely." It was at that very second that everything clicked in Devereaux's subconscious. The screams of the salon owner were commensurate with his offenses, with what he deserved. If that were true, then the screams of the men he had heard at the farm were exactly the same. Commensurate with what the men deserved. Not only could the judge now live with the screams; he could taunt them. He could make fun of them with his friend. He would figure out later how to tell Mary Jane that he had been cured. Cured, at least as far as he cared to be. In a twisted way, the day's events had the happy effect of relieving Devereaux from his mental conflict. He no longer needed to confide in anyone concerning his behavior or motives. The lawbreaking, the cruelty, and the Secret Society would all be things which the judge would handle psychologically by himself. It seemed that going forward, neither his conduct nor his conscience would get in his way and trip him up. Mr. Ralph could be trusted not to tell anyone about their unfortunate run-in with a certain judicial figure and his henchman. Fear of swift and certain reprisal would see to that. The two women hairstylists went home to their families that evening, each sporting two black eyes and very, very tight lips.

The permanent child inside Devereaux's psyche put a spring in his step as he went home to his wife to boast how he had defended her honor that afternoon. Without supplying the gory details, he cheerfully informed Jeri that Mr. Ralph and company had been thoroughly vanquished. Jeri was coming out of the shower, prominently naked with only a towel on her head.

"Thank you, my darling, dashing, Sir Walter Scott hero," she exclaimed as she planted a kiss on Jack. The judge waited for his wife to dry her hair, then perhaps to partake in a pre-dinner zesty session.

"How's your scalp diagnosis, honey?"

"It's actually quite good. She said I have nothing to worry about."

"That's a relief," said the judge. "I thought everything would be all right."

All of this good news prompted Mrs. Devereaux to share with Jack what she had been reluctant to do the previous day. "The only vain concern I have now is my weight."

"That's not a valid concern, baby, I keep telling you that."

"Aren't you sweet. But I'm afraid I'm going to be fat for a while. Fatter and fatter, if you get my drift." Jeri came out of the bathroom to witness her husband's initial reaction to announcing her pregnancy. She had found out two days prior but was mortified that she didn't mention it to Jack because she was so upset about her hair. The reason for her going to the salon in the first place was to look her best for her husband when she sprung the news to him.

Devereaux had not completely sworn off being a father, though his plate was always so full with his ambitions and schemes. It was questionable how much room was left on that plate for anything else. He managed to put a huge smile on his face for Jeri's sake the minute he was told, but he was unsure about the lifetime of responsibility that it entailed. Having gone over the possibility in his mind for many months, he was sure that he preferred a girl to a boy, unusual for a blue blood whose job it was to provide his parents with a continuing heir, perpetuating the family name. But somehow through all that pride and egoism, Jack Devereaux recoiled at the thought of raising a son to be like himself. To have to live and serve as an example every day was unsettling to him, the responsibility daunting. With a daughter, he would simply pour out love and affection on her and let his wife do the rest.

Fortunately for the lovely couple, Geraldine was pregnant with a girl. "We should name her Violet," said Jack as he hugged Jeri tightly. "It's your favorite flower and one of your signature colors."

"Wow, I can't believe it, Jack. I thought we would spend days consulting Mary Jane and your mom, talking back and forth. A name is ever so important. But I love, love, love the idea of naming her Violet! Bravo, Judge Devereaux."

"Well, apparently this is my day, isn't it? I tell you what—come to bed with me right now. And afterwords, I will blow dry your hair for you."

"Ooooh, my attentive husband. And father of my child." Jeri suddenly pushed the judge backwards. She then dove into the bed with her hair dripping wet.

"Your hair looks different this evening, Jeri," said Thomas.

"But lovely nonetheless," Corrine chimed in. Jack glanced over at Jeri, and they giggled.

"Your son was quite the hairdresser just an hour ago," said a playful Geraldine. "He dried my hair and puffed it up too much."

"Why, isn't that sweet. Thomas, you wouldn't do something like that for me for all the land in the county," Corrine said. Thomas just shook his head as he reengaged with his steak.

"I'm pregnant!" blurted out Jeri with an excitement not well contained.

Mary Jane was the first to congratulate her, leaping into Jeri's arms. Corrine joined the embrace, and while the ladies' affections and exhilaration were on full display, Thomas looked up from his dinner plate and gave Jack a "well done" nod of approval. Corrine Devereaux could expect a granddaughter to spoil. And ironically, the impending arrival of Violet Devereaux had the added effect of altering the melancholy state of affairs over the devastating loss of Courtney. Despite Jack's nervousness, the timing of this pregnancy could not have been more joyous and opportune for the Devereaux family as a whole.

Later that evening, Jack sat outside on the veranda with a Cognac, wearing an overcoat. The wintry weather was beginning to settle in, although the Piedmont sky was clear and shining a million stars. Many a man would be incapable of compartmentalizing his thoughts between love and joy on the one hand and wielding dreadful power on the other. Devereaux was not among them. He could launch a reign of terror against a beauty shop who dared offend his wife, bribe and threaten public officials, and engage in almost unpardonable cruelty against helpless criminal defendants. Yet he could still feel the same love for his family, the same adoration and gratitude for his wife and daughter-to-be, as the next guy. He could still appreciate the starry night in the country that engulfed his ancestral home. Some guys have all the luck, the saying goes.

"How are you feeling inside, little brother? Pretty big news," Mary Jane said as she snuck up behind Jack.

"Sit down, sis. I'm glad you moved back here to Bourbon Hill. You're going to be one hell of an aunt."

"I don't know about that. To tell you the truth, kids scare me sometimes."

"Join the club. I'm happy enough, and I'm elated for Jeri. But I'm scared too!"

"Of what, brother?"

"Scared that little Violet might turn out like me."

"What do you mean, Jack? Mom, Jeri, and I will make sure she doesn't take on any of your demons," she exclaimed, laughing.

Jack sipped his Cognac and turned his chair around to face Mary Jane. "I don't want her inheriting my nature, sis. I want my daughter to be like Jeri, like you."

With that, Mary Jane threw back her glass of wine and shivered. Her cheeks reddened with emotion, though disguised by the cold night air. Then her eyes teared up as she kissed Jack and thanked him for the wonderful compliment, though it was not a compliment of which she felt worthy.

CHAPTER 5

Timothy Mansfield died suddenly in his sleep at the farm he loved which he shared with his wife, Courtney. Theirs was not an ideal romantic union, but it was one that they both had agreed to settle for.

In his own way, Timothy and his parents served as an anchor of stability for the restless soul that was Courtney Devereaux. Being the apple of her father's eye only enabled her restless and willful nature, rendering her wholly unfit to fulfill her parents in any reciprocal fashion. Courtney did not have to learn her obstinate nature; she came into this world as she exited it. This may explain Thomas's and Corrine's inability to embrace Mary Jane the way they should have all those years. It may also explain why Thomas was so hard on Jack. The son was always easier for him to punish than the baby girl. Could a simple transference and psychodrama inspired by young Courtney have led to the neglect and abuse of the other two children? Abuse that propelled extra guilt on Thomas's part when he gave Bourbon Hill to Jack?

The Mansfield family doctor pronounced death at 7:30 a.m., Thursday, December 1st. The cause of his death was unofficially ruled cardiac arrest. An otherwise healthy but emotionally distraught man of 34 went to bed, and his heart simply stopped beating. He was to be buried right next to his wife in the historic family cemetery as soon as possible. An autopsy was ruled out as an "unsouthern" intrusion into the Mansfield family privacy.

Mr. and Mrs. Mansfield's determination was fueled in part by their belief that Timothy died of a broken heart, which he may indeed have.

A tragic figure, Timothy had loving parents and a proper childhood; a happy little boy he always was. He made friends easily and excelled in school and sports, even becoming one of Virginia's youngest bank presidents at age 29. He could have married any number of lovely and eligible young Piedmont ladies. But the heart wants what it wants, and poor Timothy was hopelessly in the clutches of Courtney Devereaux before their first kiss. This otherwise excellent young man unfortunately gave himself over to a woman he could never please. Absolutely nothing he said or did was ever close to good enough. Timothy had to feel the failure and disappointment every day of their marriage. The one and only exception was the day he confessed to his wife that he was rubbing out her hated brother.

In the end, we are all responsible for our actions, but do not make the mistake of holding Courtney unaccountable for transforming a decent and good-natured man into a desperate attempted murderer. Judge Devereaux had been kind and generous in his defense of his brother-in-law. More than just an excuse to spite his sister, Jack thought well of Timothy and was profoundly disturbed by his continual mistreatment at her hands. When the Devereauxs heard the tragic news, every one of them thought that Timothy had committed suicide. It was a logical conclusion to draw, given his years of unrequited love and the violent end of his young wife.

"I cannot believe the misfortune of those poor Mansfields, Jack. Your parents as well," said a sorrowful Geraldine. "He was such a young man, a good man, Jack."

"I know he was, honey. Between you and me, he deserved better than Courtney. Not saying this to be cruel, Jeri. But it's the truth. She warped him. She disintegrated the man with her indifference, her narcissism."

"Jack, honey, it's so soon after her own death, please..."

"No, Jeri. You're my wife, and you need to know how I feel about all this. She was a bitch from hell. She was a whore! And the worse kind of person as regards loyalty. She spent her whole life pissing on the very people who showed her the most love. I'm ashamed that she was ever a part of our family. And that is the final word on this. Understood?"

Jeri stood over Jack, who was seated in the parlor, and tried to mount a reply. She could not. So, the Devereaux family then did one of the things they do best—went into dinner and disengaged from all suffering and the concerns of the wider world.

The next morning was Friday, sentencing day at the Fauquier County Circuit Court. The judge banged the gavel and left his courtroom. Family members of the man he had just sentenced to life in prison were screaming and wailing. "Frank, the defendant's lawyer has a big mouth."

"I know, sir. I could hear him flapping his damn fool gums all morning. Why didn't you hold him in contempt for being disrespectful?"

"I don't exactly know. My mind was somewhere else, and he wasn't particularly bothering me." Devereaux turned toward McSherry and looked him square in the eye. "But now, I am bothered. Go back in the courtroom and bring him to me."

The judge forgot all about what was gnawing at him that morning. He drank a scotch. Then Frank came into the chambers with the lawyer. "Mr. Arnold Pennington of the American Civil Liberties Union. Have a seat."

"Sentencing is over, your honor. I was just leaving to go and prepare my appeal," said Mr. Pennington with an arrogant heir.

"There won't be one."

"What did you say, Judge?"

"There won't be an appeal filed, at least not by you."

"Now look," said Pennington as he stood up from the chair in quite the bold manner. Just then, McSherry punched him in the throat and kicked out his knee. Devereaux vacated his chair and hovered like a grizzly bear over the attorney.

"Repeat after me, Pennington. I will file no appeal in this case or indulge anyone else to do so." Pennington was on the floor, clutching his very sore knee, coughing and wheezing to get his breath. When he did, he repeated Devereaux's order verbatim. "Frank, get the man a scotch, please. You like scotch, don't you, Mr. Pennington?" The agonized lawyer nodded in the affirmative. "Now, if you do exactly as I tell you from now on, counselor, there is no reason why we can't have a cordial professional relationship."

"Yes, Judge. I understand completely."

"Good boy," said the judge as he patted the man on the back. "Good boy."

Pennington chugged his whiskey, grabbed his briefcase, and left the chambers, thoroughly compliant. "Well, that was altogether necessary," Jack said. "Changing the subject, Frank, do we have anything new on the blackmail front? Do we need to hire any new girls? I want those legislators yesterday."

"Nothing new today, sir. But I have to tell you, Judge, you're moving at bullet speed with your operations lately. I can barely keep up."

"Why wait?" inquired Devereaux. Frank smiled.

"Your meeting is coming up. What are we going to do with the Attorney General after he has served up the goodies?"

"The only sensible thing, Frank. We will run him for Governor."

Meanwhile, the Virginia legislature, true to its word (something quite out of character) passed the judicial reform law and voted to reappoint Judge Devereaux for a six-year term. It was no surprise, but he was relieved all the same. Frank had sat out the meeting with Devereaux, the Attorney General, and the other judges. At that meeting, the Society was expanded to include judges and law enforcement officials from the eastern and most populous parts of the state. The entire Commonwealth of Virginia now answered to the Society on all criminal justice matters.

"You missed a real doozy, Frank," Devereaux said. "A judge...from Virginia

Beach...asked me what name I had given our Society. I told him I knew it once, but it's so secretive that I forgot it. Ha-ha-ha!"

"Damn it, Judge, I wished I had been there," Frank laughed.

"You would have been bored to tears. No loss for you, buddy," Devereaux said.

"What are we going to do with all this power, Judge? What's our endgame?"

"The endgame is...there is no endgame. Power-grabbing is like climbing a tree. You either attain to the next level or you fall backwards. If you remain still too long, you're suspended and then you wear out. And then you fall back." Jack looked his friend in the eye with all seriousness. "There is no contingency for quitting, Frank. We may move fast, we may move slow. But we do not stop as long as there is something to get. That would be a sure-fire way to lose a big chunk of what we have already gained."

"Don't we take more and more risks if we keep this up, Judge?"

"We take a bigger risk if we stop and let other people figure us out. I'm talking multi-generational power, Frank, running the most historic state in the country; certainly one of the most important, and my home. You and I, Frank...We are becoming the government, without either of us standing for any election. And governing never ceases."

"That's right, sir. Somebody always governs."

"And why should it be anyone but us, Frank? Let me tell you a little story about a university study done here in hill country about 50 years ago. The psychologists directing the study found that the good people of southern Appalachia possessed the highest IQs of any region in the United States. Considering the propaganda out there that we are all a bunch of ignorant crackers, they repeated the tests several times. You know what happened? Same result, Frank, the same result. This means that blue bloods like me from Fauquier and the Piedmont, and you folks from the hills of Kentucky, are kindred spirits. Of the same bloodlines. Hell, we are the cagiest, most wily people anywhere. As long as we keep our heads and stay true to our ways, we can whip everybody, all the time, anywhere!"

McSherry just happily grinned, for he had nothing to add to the substantive monologue. His sensibilities were heightened, though, for he knew from a young age that he and his people were different from most other folks. He just never heard anyone put it to him so succinctly and educated-like.

"You know, Judge, it's only a matter of time before the Feds learn something involving our operations," warned Frank.

"I've been considering that possibility for a while. Do you know anyone trustworthy over at the FBI?"

"I know several good agents, Judge. But there is only one of them that I can guarantee will play ball."

"Then it's him we want, right, Frank?"

"Actually, sir, it's *her*."

The judge's eyes lit up suddenly. "You know what? Good," he said.

"Good?" replied Frank. "You'd rather deal with a lady than a man?"

"In our case, Frank, yes I would. Think about it. All the slippery fucks we've had to deal with at the state and local level are men. Politicians! We keep having to re-bribe and re-threaten them again and again. Conversely, the one and only time I made a deal with a woman politician was a most honorable exchange of illegalities. I bought a deal from her, and she stayed bought. Now that's integrity, Frank!"

McSherry listened intently to the judge's reasoning and again was impressed to the point of being dumbfounded. And he still could not bring himself to call Devereaux by his fist name, despite being invited do so on many an occasion.

"Approach her gently and find out what her current needs and weaknesses are. Money should be enough this time, for women are much more practical than most men, Frank."

"Yes, Judge."

"Is she in the Washington Field Office or Headquarters?"

"Headquarters, which is the best place to keep secrets and halt investigations."

"I'd like to meet her as soon as possible," ordered Devereaux. "Get it done."

CHAPTER 6

Violet Savannah Devereaux was born on June 4th, a healthy baby from a healthy mother who had enjoyed a pregnancy free of complications. The parents were ecstatic, the aunt was happy, the grandparents were all happy. Geraldine's parents had visited her separately during the pregnancy and promised to be in town for the Christening of the child in September. Thomas and Corrine enjoyed great relief, for circumstances had threatened their dream of a third generation of Devereauxs living at Bourbon Hill. Not only had Jack not put up a fight, but he came to embrace his impending fatherhood quickly after Jeri had announced she was pregnant. New life had opened the windows at the Devereaux estate, bringing in fresh air, excitement, and great anticipation for the future.

Thomas had become more of a recluse in his older age, keeping to himself and only interacting with the family at dinner and special events. He had been ensconced in his library of over 7,000 volumes, determined to live out his remaining days as an author of something distinguished. He had of yet been unable to produce any ideas for the project, adding to the man's substantial cantankerousness. The arrival of his granddaughter, however, was like a shot of cortisone for the old man. Upon holding Violet for the first time, Thomas instantly forgot his mixed emotions about wanting a grandson. Corrine had a new favorite in the house, and a happier, more doting grandma never before existed.

Jack and Geraldine had given his parents a very great gift, enhancing their present circumstances and in all probability lengthening their lives. Joy, like gratitude, is the pinnacle of emotions. It overcomes adversity and it heals like no other. All that is required is to know how to receive it as a gift. True joy is never earned and seldom deserved. Corrine understood this innately, hence her beautiful and magnanimous nature. Thomas nearly completed his life without understanding what his wife had always known. Fortunately, his son and daughter-in-law gave him another chance to partake in true joy and he took it. Bourbon Hill was a very, very happy place that summer.

An added effect for the judge was that his father was so emerged in the life of little Violet that he had entirely neglected the legal chit chats with his son, which sometimes occurred daily. Jack was stepping up his game with the Society and only wanted to jawbone the details with Frank McSherry and a very few select cohorts. Devereaux had also been secretly buying up land with cash deals from profits from the Society's ill deeds. He owned Bourbon Hill and the next farm over, where the McSherrys operated, giving him nearly 3,000 contiguous acres. This was an enormous amount of land given the less-than-two-hour proximity to Washington, D.C. Jack had also amassed thousands more acres of land abutting the Shenandoah National Park and the George Washington National Forest. This was desirable to him because nobody could build in the National Parks and Forests. It felt like having exponentially more unspoilable land free of charge, and also of taxes. Happy is the man who owns the ground upon which he walks! No proverbial notion is more fundamentally American than that. With the raw legal and political prowess he had now amassed, coupled with his magnificent estate and newly acquired lands, Jack Devereaux had as much wealth, power, and prestige as an English Baronet. And he wasn't finished.

"Jack, did you read the papers this morning? My goodness, a registered sex offender just blocks away from our Warrenton house was found dead in his home. Throat cut. And castrated," Jeri winced and shivered as she told her husband as he was shaving.

"Don't ask me to feel bad for the man, honey. I know the case well. Back before I was shot, this...man ran a child robbery ring. He took poor kids, trained them as pickpockets and shoplifters. He came before me, and I sentenced him to life in prison because he had threatened these kids and their families with violence. Some months later, that nitwit of a Governor commuted his sentence, and he was released last year. Now, we find out that he was molesting the young boys." Devereaux peeked out of the bathroom with a face full of lather as Geraldine tossed the paper in the trash can and sipped some dazzlingly delicious French coffee.

She then stared at Jack and began teasing herself as he disappeared into the bathroom. Little Violet was sleeping soundly, and Mrs. Devereaux was profoundly in a state of lust for her husband. She had been extra randy ever since the baby had been born. Just watching him shave with nothing but a towel on set her off, and the judge could've had himself a real treat; instead, he opened his mouth again. "I just hope whoever iced that piece of shit used a dull, rusty knife."

Jeri's hands dropped to her side, her hormones not yet settled from the last several months. She breathed deeply and returned to the coffee. She wasn't upset with Jack, but that last comment killed the mood for her. Any talk of violence was usually a put-off for her, especially flippant remarks about violence. Though Devereaux understood his wife quite well, he struggled with this particular thing. After all, violence was a regular part of his routine. If he couldn't share some of his feelings on the subject with his wife, then who?

The strong coffee aside, Geraldine fell asleep in her Shay's Lounge. Jack dressed and walked over to her and kissed her forehead. As he passed the kitchen on his way out, there sat Mary Jane at the table.

"Jack, please come to my office tomorrow afternoon. I think we need a close-out session, what with everything that's been happening."

"Can't we just a have a drink here and talk in private? I have a busy week, and I don't want to drive all the way to Charlottesville."

"Please, Jack, I'll treat us to dinner afterwards. I need the privacy, dear brother, I have something I want to tell you, too," she said with moist eyes and a longing stare.

"All right, sis. I can meet you at 4 p.m." Mary Jane's heightened good mood was set for the next 24 hours. She hugged and kissed her brother with a little more intensity than normal, then let him go as he was late for court.

The judge put in a long day of motions, pre-trial and scheduling activity, and read close to 200 pages of briefs. When 4:30 rolled around, he was ready to imbibe. "Do you believe in God, Frank?"

McSherry sat down in Devereaux's chambers, starting in on his second scotch. "Well, sir. Me and the rest of the boys were brought up Baptist."

"I'm Episcopalian," Devereaux politely interrupted. "My question is, do you believe in God?"

Frank leaned back in his chair and scratched his head, thinking about the question. "In my part of the country, most folks seem to take it for granted that God is real and there is a hereafter. I've never really questioned it, I guess."

Devereaux stared at Frank for a long moment. He loved this man as a friend, a confidante, and a colleague. He approved of Frank's character in every way, but even for Devereaux it was a struggle to reconcile the sterling qualities of the McSherrys with the ease in which they committed their barbarities.

Lumping himself in with the McSherrys, he was attempting to reconcile his spiritual sense with the ease in which he himself had ordered and sanctioned these very cruelties. McSherry could see the puzzled and distressed look on Devereaux's face and pieced the whole mood of the room together, as though he were both philosopher and psychologist. "Judge, I was reading a biography of Oliver Cromwell the other week. You know, the English Parliament fellow who had King Charles beheaded?"

"Indeed I do, Frank. My mother says we're related to him. His children migrated to Culpeper."

"Anyway, Judge. Cromwell, at the end of the civil war in England, had described his action as a 'cruel necessity.' Ever since that book, I've been contemplating that piece of our business. I think that these things we do can be chalked up to cruel necessity."

Devereaux sat motionless for the next minute. He could not have said what needed to be said any better himself. He was simultaneously impressed with Frank and displeased with himself for having to be told what was so obvious. But he was relieved, nonetheless. The legitimate and legal governments of Virginia and of every other state commit acts of cruelty. They put men to death, sentence men to the horrible conditions of prison life. Now, the Society was becoming the real power in Virginia. Cruel necessity was simply a part of dispensing justice properly. Devereaux left the courthouse for Bourbon Hill, looking forward to kissing his wife and holding his baby daughter. He was thoroughly appeased and solidified in his self-satisfaction, but he was unsure whether or not he believed in God.

CHAPTER 7

"How can you not believe that there is a wonderful God in heaven? Just look at her, honey," Jeri proclaimed to her husband, now the doting father. "She's just God's perfect little gift, is she not?"

"She's wonderful! Spectacular!" The judge gently snatched Violet from Jeri's arms and sat down on the sofa with her. He loved nothing so much as being with his wife and their bundle of joy and happiness. Jack was so playful that he bonded with his daughter easily. He even changed a diaper now and then. But very soon, Corrine had to come to the rescue to stand in for Jack concerning the midnight awakenings and feedings. As a working judge, Devereaux declared that he must sleep through the night. And as much he adored his little girl, he participated in none of the sleepless night sufferings the next few months.

The next day, Devereaux was determined not to drive down to his sister's office. He had the nerve to tell her that the baby had kept him up all night. "Meet me in the small parlor at home tonight at 9 p.m. We'll have a drink and talk then, okay?"

Mary Jane answered yes, and Jack hung up the phone.

"I have to be in court in 30 minutes, Frank. I'm curious, which one ripped the balls off of our friendly neighborhood child molester?"

"That would be cousin number three, Judge," Frank said.

"He sure is the meanest of the three, isn't he, Frank?"

"He is definitely open for business, sir."

"I assume the police won't find anything?"

"Only some DNA from one of the foreign national gang members, who just happens to be sitting right here in the jail. I arrested him yesterday."

"Frank, you didn't."

"Consider it a present, Judge, what with you being a new father and such." Devereaux was pleased and touched at his right-hand man's thoughtfulness. "I even made sure the clerk draws your name for the trial," Frank continued.

"Let's see, I will find the man guilty of a crime he didn't commit, and we will send him down to the Buchanan County farm. Meanwhile, the real killer gets away. All in a day's work, Frank. Anything else before I take the bench?"

"Our friend in the FBI got promoted the other day."

Devereaux looked troubled. "She's not being transferred?"

"No, sir. She now supervises the people who do her old job. Makes it twice as easy for her to take care of us."

Jack laughed. "Can you believe life can be this good, Frank? All this planning and engineering, and it's these lucky breaks that push us so far ahead."

"Let's hope they keep coming our way, Judge."

"Frank, I will remind myself every day to place us in the path of good fortune."

"Before you go, Judge, I need to explain a detail to you." Devereaux motioned for McSherry to continue. "90 percent, maybe more, of the folks in our Society are either trustworthy friends, amongst the blackmailed and bribed, or some combination of the above. The few outliers are the ones most likely to sing. That's why me and the fellows have allowed them to believe that we'll kill them if they do talk. What is your position on this, Judge?"

Devereaux sat quietly, tapping a pen on his desk. He swung his chair to the right and looked out the only window in his office. The blinds were open. Then he breathed deeply and swung back to look at McSherry. "Let them believe that their breaking silence could be fatal. In fact, remind them from time to time. But if someone does talk, we will handle it with much effective treachery, but no killing. I told someone I love not long ago that I never harm innocent people. I mean to keep that word, Frank."

"I hear you, Judge. Back in my Army days, I harmed people that didn't really have it coming. Doesn't feel very good, sir."

"Well, then we're on the same page as usual, Frank."

At dinner that evening, Jack took Violet to the dining room over the objections of nobody. As far as her grandparents and father were concerned, she had the run of the place. Were it not for the tightly disciplined parenting of Geraldine, this little girl would grow up impossibly spoiled. The judge travelled through the family dinner with one hand on his fork and wine glass, the other tickling Violet as she lay in Geraldine's arms. Everyone was content, everyone relaxed—except for Mary Jane, whose nervousness she hid well from the rest of the family. She did not eat very much, just sat there quietly with a false smile on her face, counting the minutes until her 9 p.m. meeting with Jack. A few minutes before the appointed time, Thomas excused himself to retire to his study. Corrine and Geraldine were already upstairs with Violet, and Jack went to the parlor bar to pour himself something considerably stronger than the dinner wine.

"I'll fire up the heater on the veranda, Mary Jane. Go get your coat," Jack said. The siblings sat down outside for that all-important private meeting. Not knowing what to expect, Jack started in. "Well, sis. First off, I want to thank you for the sessions and for helping me get over my problem."

"Are you over it, little brother?"

"Yes. You helped a great deal. But something snapped inside my head not long ago; it made me realize that my problem is no longer a problem."

Mary Jane locked eyes with her brother. "Are you quite sure this is not just wishful thinking?" she asked caringly.

"Yes, Mary Jane, quite."

Mary Jane began to shake. Jack initially thought it was the cold. But when tears began to stream down her cheeks, he knew that this night was going to be all about her.

"Do you have something you need to get off your chest, sis?" Jack pulled her chair tightly against his and hugged her with his right arm. "You've been a good doctor to me these few weeks. But you obviously need your brother tonight. Tell me what's wrong."

Mary Jane took a drink and leaned her head on Jack's shoulder. She then took nearly half an hour to recount their entire relationship, how they were even more than brother and sister. "Remember when I would be out on a date, and you would stay up and wait for me to come home with tears in your eyes? Oh, that was special, Jack, so very, very special. To be truthful, I couldn't wait to get home and kiss you goodnight, hug you to sleep."

"I will never forget those nights, Mary Jane. There I was, a jealous little boy, and...Well, it was so very, very special," Jack agreed. "But our history together is beautiful. Our relationship now is beautiful. What's bothering you?"

"I killed Courtney," declared Mary Jane as she squeezed Jack's hand ferociously.

The judge knotted up inside despite the large amount of liquor in his system. He was quite alert at that moment but strangely controlled. "What do you mean, Mary Jane?"

"I have a patient who is...competent in such matters. When I overheard you telling Frank McSherry that Courtney was responsible for your shooting, I...I decided then and there that she had to go. Oh, Jack, my sweet boy." With that, Mary Jane led her stunned brother inside the house and into a private sitting room off the kitchen. She closed the door and dragged her brother onto the sofa, where she attacked him with the fiercest embrace.

Desperately trying to make both of them feel the love, Mary Jane pulled Jack's head to her bosom and cradled him, as she had so many times before, when he was little.

By that point, Jack was an emotional pretzel. Tied up inside like never before, he struggled to keep silent as he formulated his inner monologue. "Tell me everything, Mary Jane, now."

"Well, my patient stalked her for days, weeks, and then when she took the drive on Deep Gorge Road, he ran her off the highway at the most dangerous point. Oh, Jack, I was there when you were shot. You almost died. And that evil little witch. I had to do it, you see. I had to! Oh, Jack, my sweet boy. My sweet, sweet angel." She kissed and caressed her brother, crying and hugging him close. Mary Jane was so overwhelmed with her own emotions that she utterly failed to recognize Jack's tears.

This news was a double gut punch for him. Not only was the sister he worshiped a killer, but she had not heard the whole aforesaid conversation. Had she continued to eavesdrop, she would have understood that Tim Mansfield was the real mastermind of his attempted murder. But he could not dare tell Mary Jane that she had made such a grievous error. "I understand and appreciate your motivation, sis. Believe me, I do. This will have to be our secret, sweetheart. Do you understand? You and I have to keep quiet and take this one to the grave," he exclaimed.

His sister sniffled, rubbed her eyes, and nodded in the affirmative.

Protecting Mary Jane from the awful truth would save her but add to Jack's already overburdened and lonely conscience. There was simply nothing to do but hug and hold his sister. The two held each other so tightly that a crowbar could hardly pry them apart. They fell asleep in each other's arms and were awakened an hour later by a baby's crying. Geraldine had gotten up to rescue Violet from her lonely crib and thought it a good idea to walk her around the house. As she passed by the little sitting room, she could see through the glass door her husband cuddled up on the sofa with his sister.

Jeri assumed the best-case scenario—Jack and Mary Jane confiding in one another about Jack's dreams and related issues, and expressing appropriate love and comfort toward each other.

Jack laid Mary Jane down and put a blanket over her. Then he followed his wife and daughter into the kitchen. "Well, your therapy suggestion worked better than you thought, Jeri."

"Really?" exclaimed a pleased Geraldine. "How so?"

"Mary Jane helped me identify and surmount what was behind my dreams. Then, tonight, she confided in me about some family emotions she had been carrying for years. Stuff I never knew about. And I ended up treating her. Isn't that crazy?" Jack asked as he scrambled for a believable explanation.

Jeri just smiled and rocked Violet to sleep. The judge desperately wanted to go to bed himself, but there was another matter to attend to. He went back to the little parlor and gently woke Mary Jane, telling her he had to know the name and address of the man she paid to kill Courtney. "I know you have your professional ethics, but for your own protection, sis, trust me. I have to know." Mary Jane complied, and Jack went to bed.

The next morning before breakfast, Devereaux placed the proper phone call, then went downstairs to join his family. Due to the fatigue from the previous night, he lingered at breakfast and drank an entire pot of coffee himself. Mary Jane was asleep in her bedroom. Thomas and Corrine just assumed that their ragged-looking son had been up half the night with the baby. Geraldine had not disturbed Corrine the night before. She took care of her daughter by herself. Geraldine ate a small amount, breastfed Violet, and then the two went back upstairs for a hopefully long nap. Jack went to the courthouse, very late. As he drove down the breathtaking driveway of Bourbon Hill, the cold and sunny morning placed his mind in a state of hyper alertness. The heaviness of the prior evening had been so intense and the circumstances so remarkable that he no longer had a confidante in his sister, concerning the whole episode with Courtney.

The judge had decided that even though Tim Mansfield had been thoroughly pacified by his forced meeting with himself and Sergeant McSherry, Mansfield would forever remain a loose end which at some point would have to be tied. So, on his orders, two of the McSherry cousins had slipped into the Mansfield home in the middle of the night and into the separate bedroom where Tim slept alone. One cousin hovered above the bed with a pillow ready to pounce while the other one carefully stuck Mansfield's ankle with a syringe. Tim never awakened so the cousins left the scene speedily but carefully. The ultra-sophisticated chemical compound put Mansfield into extreme cardiac arrest. If he ever achieved consciousness, he showed no signs of having done so.

"How I wish I could tell Mary Jane what I did to Tim," Jack said to himself as he neared the courthouse. "But I cannot, not ever. She thinks my shooting was all Courtney's fault, and she must never think otherwise. Not for her sake or for mine." As Devereaux settled in his office, Frank was already there. He handed Frank a small piece of paper.

"The usual, Judge?"

"Yes, the usual." Devereaux prepared for a trial that threatened to dominate his week. He asked his secretary for more coffee as McSherry departed. Jack was beginning to lose passion for his main job. Trials, civil procedure, and judicial professionalism were small things, next to the Society and his power plays. In no time at all, Judge Devereaux and the few people he trusted had created an alternative state. He had achieved remarkable power on his own, but the Society allowed him to mettle in the affairs of any public, political, or consequential business concern in Virginia.

He didn't need the money for himself, but he took as much as he could. Julius Caesar once wrote that the principal quality of an effective statesman is foresight, the ability to see around the corner where few people can. Devereaux was brutally efficient in this regard, and this foresight told him that maintaining power would require an insane amount of money at his disposal. That very week, he took a recess from his trial and read in the papers that the Director of the FBI was retiring. The President was just beginning the process of looking for a replacement. Immediately, Devereaux's mind went to work. The FBI Director, appointed by the President of the United States and confirmed by the United States Senate, serves a 10-year term.

"Frank, our friend over at the FBI would be the first woman to serve as Director, wouldn't she?"

"Yes, sir, I believe she would."

"Will you ask if she wants the job? I will make some calls and see what it will require."

The two met the following afternoon in the judge's chambers.

Frank knew the answer before he asked the Special Agent and Supervisor. The judge was told by his friend in the National Party that $5 million would spread around the right influence to get her nominated by the White House. Another $5 million would ensure Senate confirmation.

"10 million bucks for 10 years, Frank. Seems a fair trade."

"And she wants the job, Judge."

"Excellent. This will keep the Feds out of our affairs for a decade. Not a bad insurance policy." Devereaux grinned and then grimaced. He had 10 minutes to get back on the bench and listen to a devastatingly boring trial. "Before I go, Frank, is that other matter disposed of?" McSherry quickly relayed the events of the prior three days to Devereaux. He and McSherry Cousin Number Three went to Albemarle County. Deputy Moses of the Sheriff's Department entered his cottage late in the day. As he took off his gun belt and heavy jacket, the deputy realized that his front door had been unlocked.

As he went for his gun, a crashing blow to the cheek forced him into an easy chair. The cousin grabbed him from behind the neck and held him for Frank, who displayed his pistol, pointing it at the Deputy's head. "You're no longer a patient of Mary Jane Devereaux. You never did her bidding. Courtney

Mansfield's death was an accident. And the judge has a present for you."

The deputy tried to yell for help, and Cousin Number Three shoved a rag into his mouth. Frank put the pistol to his head and pulled the trigger. *Click!* The terrified officer nearly fainted with relief. "Take this favor, Deputy. The judge only offers his good graces once. And remember, nothing ever gets back to Mary Jane Devereaux, or else next time you won't see my face." The deputy was released, and when he caught his breath, he was all compliance.

"I think he got the message, Judge," Frank said.

"Good work, Frank. But another loose end. Why take a chance?"

"I can control this one, Judge. The more cops we own, the better."

Devereaux was finally swayed by McSherry's last remark. And he was happy not to have to kill this man. Mansfield had been a loose end as well, but a loose end that had tried to murder him. Deputy Moses was pliable. He would cooperate out of fear and in favor of money.

CHAPTER 8

The weekend was a great relief to the judge. His trial was over, loose ends had been tied up, and he could spend long hours relaxing with Geraldine and Violet, which was why he appeared to be disturbed when his wife announced that Frank McSherry was driving through the black iron gate up the driveway to see him.

"I'll be in the small parlor, honey. Send him in." Devereaux poured two scotches and sat down waiting for Jeri to show Frank in.

"I'm sorry to bother you on the weekend, sir. But I have good news I want to share and a favor to ask you." Devereaux handed Frank a drink and the Sergeant got right to the point. "I asked Mimi to marry me last night, and she said yes."

"Frank, that's the best news I've heard since our FBI coup. Congratulations," said the judge as he toasted with Frank.

"Both Mimi and I want you to perform the ceremony. Would that be too much to ask?"

"Why, not at all. I'd be honored."

"Thank you, Judge. That means much to us."

"Why don't you and Mimi come out here for supper Sunday night. A little pre-celebration."

"Thanks, Judge. You know, I never thought I would be this happy. I mean,

I've been with a lot of ladies, but I've never loved one before. I just can't imagine growing old without her."

"I know what you mean. That's how you know she's the one, if you can't do without her." Devereaux poured more whiskey, and the two gentlemen drank and chatted like fraternity brothers. "I heard from my Washington contact, Frank. Constance will be confirmed FBI Director by voice vote in the Senate next Friday."

"Damn, sir. That's just about the luckiest thing to happen to us since...the beginning," exhorted McSherry with a bit of solemnity in his voice.

"A whole decade of federal protection. Empires have risen and fallen in less time," said Devereaux in a philosophical vane.

The next day, Geraldine commandeered her husband to spend his Saturday watching Violet so she and Corrine could spend the day at a spa and take in some shopping. Surprisingly, it was a welcome duty for the judge. He had a desire to wax literary that day and needed a captive audience. As the little one cried out in the afternoon, Devereaux retrieved her from the crib, gave her a change, and walked her throughout the main level of the house. As she began to calm, he reached for the whiskey and sat down in the little parlor with her. The liquor took immediate effect, and Jack began to softly lecture his baby girl.

"The world is a toilet, little one. Well, at least the wider, densely populated world. But you are lucky to be born into this family, at this estate, in this wonderful place we call the Virginia Piedmont. I wish you could see the beautiful meadow and the snow-covered hills in the backdrop. Such beauty! Such tranquility. We live in a wondrous oasis, sweetheart."

Little Violet burped and coughed as she desperately tried to stretch out her tiny arms. The gesture was so endearingly cute, it knocked Devereaux off his train of thought. He had to drink more to regain it.

"An oasis, daughter. An oasis in a desert of shit. Horrible people in awful lands in terrible cities. You see, that's daddy's main job in life. To keep the filth out of our oasis. To contain and control the masses of people far too close to our paradise and make them either serve us or leave us alone. But that's me, honey. I want something different for you, something better. I do what I have to do out of necessity, for control over things. Your life and job will be inspired by your mama and your grandma! Aunt Mary Jane, even. I'm your father, Violet, but they will nurture you to be the wonderful young lady I know you will be. You will probably marry someone. I hope it's someone like Frank. A good protector, a man of strength, values and honor." Devereaux opened another pint of bourbon and drank. "I will always be there for you, child. Nothing and no one will ever hurt you while I stand guard. I love you more than I can say, Violet." He kissed her head gently. "I want you to love your old man, but I pray you don't grow up to be him."

Devereaux had exhausted his words. He spent the next two hours sipping spirits and staring out at the horizon. When Geraldine softly entered the parlor room, she was overcome by the tender scene. Father and daughter were sound asleep. She would have needed a team of horses to pry Violet from Jack's arms.

CHAPTER 9

Y ou are a good person, Mary Jane. The best!" Judge Devereaux declared.

"How can you say that, dear brother? After what I've done. She was family!" Mary Jane sagged into the sofa, drinking wine from a very large goblet.

"Courtney may technically be your victim, but she was a rotten person from the very beginning. You and I both know that."

Mary Jane motioned for Jack to sit down beside her. As he did, she placed her glass on the table and hugged him tightly. "*You* are a good person, Jack. Don't ever think that you're not."

"You do me too much honor, sis. I'm good where it is easy to be good. I love my family, my friends, our estates, and the land around them. Hell, I'm a man of exceptionally elevated principles. But my daily life ethics are subterranean."

"You sound as though you're proud of that, Jack."

"It's the way it has to be, or else I couldn't do my job right."

"You mean being a judge?"

Jack paused. "Now Mary Jane, we've already been through this."

"Oh, yes, I forgot. The Society."

"It's probably best you don't use that word for a while."

"For how long?"

"Until I say so."

The judge was relaxed being alone with his older sister. They were alone in the house for the afternoon. He poured them each another goblet of wine and they enjoyed a few moments of silence. Mary Jane then took to reminding her brother that he took an oath to do justice to all persons at his swearing-in ceremony as a judge. Devereaux became unusually impatient toward his sister. "Sometimes there is a sharp difference between the saying of something and the meaning it."

Somehow, Mary Jane's mind had transported her toward the person she had always been, before she had her sister murdered. "So, you don't actually believe in equal justice before the law, brother?"

"No," he said with a stoic face. "Need I remind you that you don't, either." The two siblings looked at each other and then looked away for many minutes. "I promise not to allude to your deed again, Mary Jane. You know I don't mind debating with you, but don't provoke."

A much-corrected Mary Jane revisited her wine glass, and the pair avoided any possible offense to the other for the rest of the time.

Jack's thoughts wandered to the previous Sunday's dinner in honor of Frank and Mimi's nuptials. Mimi seemed to be deliriously happy with Frank. There was none of the usual secretive flirtation towards himself. Devereaux was elated, mostly for Frank. He was determined that the friend who served him so effectively, so faithfully without question, should be rewarded by having everything a man needed to be happy and fulfilled. As he performed their wedding ceremony the following day, Devereaux was most contented. He knew in his heart of hearts that he had made a match that would last and satisfy both parties well.

"You know, Judge, looking over this horizon from Bourbon Hill all these years, sharing some good drink with you...Why, that may be the best perk about being your employee. Excepting Mimi, of course!"

"Why, that's quite a compliment, Frank. And I know exactly how you feel. Sitting here with a good scotch and this Blue Ridge view and no pain-in-the-ass close neighbors makes me feel I like a haven't a care in the world. Hopefully, I never will again. I can't shake the feeling, though."

"What feeling is that, sir?"

"The feeling that something is missing. For at least 10 more years, I control society, thanks in part to your friend Constance. Hell, Frank, I am society! At least in Virginia. But now that I have everything I want, that we've done everything we have set out to do, I seem to want more. I just cannot figure out what it is."

Frank sipped some whiskey and participated in the lengthy pause in the conversation with Devereaux. A villainous grin suddenly appeared on his face as he looked over at the judge. "We are still relatively young men," he said. "Why don't we take over Kentucky?"

Devereaux twitched his head and hands as if violently startled but regained his composure within seconds. "Damn, Frank, it appears that hanging out with me all this time has turned you into a visionary." The judge sipped, Frank sipped, and then the two toasted one another in an act of friendship and admiration. Then they laughed.

EPILOGUE

Seven Years Hence

"The Past is never dead; it's not even Past."
— WILLIAM FAULKNER

Life in Fauquier County hasn't much changed. Some judges and politicians have come and gone. Shops and small businesses still line the streets of Warrenton, including Mr. Ralph, who still does hair the same, only he has slightly amended his no-refund policy. Geraldine sold her house in town and purchased two historical homes for Inns with fine dining, both of which have turned a healthy profit and been accepted with high praise by the local folks. All the same historical places and markers worthy of reverence remain in full force. Bourbon Hill stands the test of time, as stately as any building and land in the county. Everything from the black iron gate to the pond where waterfowl bed down and eagles and hawks swoop and spy their prey to the love affair between the grand estate and the mysterious morning mist and fog always selectively partial to Devereaux lands rolls in and abates with the same deliberate speed.

The immortal McSherry boys still roam the hills of Virginia and Kentucky, hunting and acquiring land with money they make from ridding Judge Devereaux's dominion of its wretched refuse. Oh, to command such a brutal and efficient force! Since before the United States came into being, the McSherry clan was securing the frontier and had fought in all of our wars.

Never had a McSherry fallen in combat. No McSherry had ever lost a fight or been anyone's victim. They all seemed to die old and of natural causes.

Frank and his clan, serving the brilliant designs of Judge Devereaux, played no small part in keeping life here in the Virginia Piedmont unchanged and durable. They continued to suck out the undesirable elements of society like a giant vacuum cleaner at the direction of Devereaux and the Secret Society. Those parts of Virginia that could not conform to the judge's Fauquier County standards were at least pacified. Nearly 1,000 violent offenders, already in the prison system or awaiting their due process, died terrible deaths at either one of the Society's farms. Hundreds more were deported under the orders of the FBI Director.

Most astonishing was the fact that nobody in the loop broke ranks or talked. The judge built his Society based upon his unmatched ability to read people, to size up their psyches and determine their motivations. His accuracy in this endeavor was downright mystical. No secret enterprises are without a shelf life, and Devereaux knew this as well. He would continue to plot and scheme with his few trusted mates in order to stay well ahead of unexpected contingencies.

Compared to the metropolis to the east, Fauquier County lived as fairytale. Looking for evil in this place was like sifting sand from a beach. And yet, when the mood for storytelling hits some of the locals up in the northwest hills, more than a few say that in that most peaceful part of the county you can hear a distant shriek now and again. Especially when that unexplained fog rises, then disappears into the dusk.

One very fine day, the Baron of Bourbon Hill kissed his wife and daughter goodbye and departed for the courthouse. Geraldine helped Violet into her newly pressed school uniform and led her downstairs. It was Aunt Mary Jane's turn to take Violet to school, a duty she treasured. Thomas and Corrine had placed a tray of donuts on the kitchen table for their favorite little scholar. Little Miss Violet was hugged, kissed, and mauled by her family on her way to school. The grandparents showered the girl with affection just by pure love and instinct. They were also, even if unwittingly, preparing their granddaughter for a life of constant love, affection, and acceptance—something they had not consistently done with their own children.

In a schoolhouse atop a small hill at the edge of a forest, an unusually beautiful and vivacious second-grade girl was yawning in class out of boredom. She couldn't wait until school adjourned for the afternoon so she could go home to Bourbon Hill and ride her pony. The teacher had just one more assignment for the youngsters, and that was to complete the American history lessons for the week by having each pupil tell the class which historical figures they admired and why. Little Violet Devereaux raised her hand.

"Yes, Violet?" invited the teacher.

"My name is Violet Devereaux, and my daddy is a judge. He is ever so important. I want to grow up and be just like him."

ABOUT THE AUTHOR

John Hilton is a novelist and historian, whose literary interests focus on the English and American Novel and the histories of classical civilization, Renaissance Europe, and the United States. Particular attention is paid to America's founding period and the American Revolution. John lives in Arlington, Virginia, where he grew up. His website is JohnHiltonNovels.com.

THE HARLOT
OF GLOUCESTER

With the 250th anniversary of the Declaration of Independence coming next summer, please celebrate in part by reading John's third book, *The Harlot of Gloucester,* coming soon! Read about people and places in and around Yorktown, Virginia, where we Americans won our independence and became a nation.